THE LUNCH GIRLS

by
Leigh Curran

SAMUEL FRENCH, INC.

45 WEST 25TH STREET   NEW YORK 10010
7623 SUNSET BOULEVARD HOLLYWOOD 90046
LONDON   TORONTO

IMPORTANT ADVERTISING NOTE

THE LUNCH GIRLS by Leigh Curran was first presented at the Long Wharf Theatre in New Haven, Conneticut, November 17 to December 18, 1977. The production was directed by Arvin Brown, settings by David Jenkins, costumes by Bill Walker, lighting by Ronald Wallace, Production Stage Manager – Anne Keefe, Production Associate – Leon Gagliardi. The cast was as follows:

in order of appearance:

CLARE .... Pamela Payton-Wright
KATE .... Leigh Curran
CHARLENE .... Suzanne Lederer
DANUSHA........................ Carol Androsky
VICKY .... Phyllis Somerville
RHONDA......................... Susan Sharkey
EDIE.............................. Carol Willard
CHEF........................ Stephen D. Newman
HENRI .... Philip Polito
JESUS .... Octavio Ciano

THE LUNCH GIRLS is dedicated to
Edward Herrmann,
Arvin Brown
and
Michael Weller
for their sensitive encouragement
of
an unknown quantity.

AUTHOR'S NOTES

Jesus, the bus boy, uses the Spanish pronunciation of his name — Hey-*zous* ... as opposed to Jesus, as in Christ. The latter, more familiar, pronunciation of the word is, however, used on page 76 where Clare uses it as an exclamation.

The late girl is the lunch girl who stays until the first girl comes to work — usually about 4:30.

The first girl is the first night girl who comes to work, although sometimes a lunch girl would substitute for her, working from 10 AM until 1 or 2 at night, with an hour break for dinner.

A night girl is a waitress who only serves cocktails and sings with the piano player — usually one or three songs in a limited repertoire. She is paid to be glamorous and helpless and earns a lot of money doing it.

THE LUNCH GIRLS
by
Leigh Curran
ACT I

Time: October, 1969. The entire action of the play takes place in the girls locker room and kitchen of a key club in mid-town Manhattan. The building is an old, rundown brownstone. The club has seen better days.

The girls are waitresses. They wear short costumes -- rhinestone straps, bustles -- with a gay nineties feel to them; opera hose, spiked platform heels and tiaras. Some girls put sequins on their faces with Elmer's glue and glitter their hair.

Their work load is the same as that of any professional waiter in spite of their conditions. They carry their own trays, bus their own tables and run themselves just as ragged.

The locker room is the setting for the first and third acts. It is in the basement. It is low-ceilinged -- cramped -- water pipes overhead and rats in the walls. The upstage wall is makeshift ... probably nothing more than sound proofing. It separates the girls from the boys. The lockers are wooden, narrow, battered -- most of the locks have been pried or broken off.

U.S. is a bathroom -- a small sink; a broken towel dispenser with a mirror in it. To the left of the sink is the stall for the john. Upstage center is the only entrance and exit, a poorly fitted wooden door that leads to the stairway into the kitchen.

CLARE enters. She is in her late twenties, drained; she wears boots, a down parka, blue jeans and a man's button-down shirt, several sizes too big and faded from use. She puts her jacket and bag in her locker and moves to the bench to clean up the mess left by the night girls. She mutters to herself and spots a bag of jelly beans. She picks it up and rummages through it.

CLARE. These are disgusting. *(She stacks some glasses, cigarette butts and leftover bits of cheese and bread on a liquor tray and exits through the door upstage center and up the stairs into the kitchen.)*

(A few beats go by. A Kleenex falls out of a hole in the upstage wall. For a moment a few fingers are visible ... then an eye peeking into the room. CLARE re-enters with a waterglass full of coffee. She crosses to the bench center stage and sits. KATE enters in a flap. She is about twenty-four; long-waisted, flat-chested ... all arms and legs.)

KATE. Guess what? I'm late, girl. Wouldn't you know it? I knew this would happen. I just knew it.

CLARE. Where's Jeanette?

KATE. She called in sick. Can you beat that? Today of all days. Just my luck. It isn't enough that I had to set up Vicky's station for the fortieth time ... no ... Stefan has to go and make me late girl, as well. Just because I was standing next to the phone. Can you help me?

CLARE. I'm working tonight.

KATE. Well, I don't know what I'm supposed to do. I've got that audition. I've got to get out of here ... I'm perfect for the part. Saint Joan ... you know.

CLARE. Did you ask Danusha?

KATE. She isn't feeling well and she's got somewhere to go. Do you have any gum?

CLARE. In my bag.

KATE. Are you sure you can't help me?

CLARE. I told you---I'm working.

KATE. Well, I don't know how you do it. Don't you ever get tired?

(CLARE shrugs.)

KATE. I mean, why are you killing yourself?

CLARE. Well, it's something to do, isn't it?

(DANUSHA enters. She is plain, peasant-like. She carries a ratty overcoat — hangs it on a flimsy hanger on the door of her locker and watches it fall to the floor. She sighs and exits into the john.)

KATE. *(Scrounges in CLARE'S bag.)* What's this?

CLARE. Oh, just a book.

KATE. Recipes. What are you doing with all these recipes?

CLARE. I keep thinking I'm going to start organizing them...you know, for when we start the restaurant.

KATE. Oh, right...the restaurant.

CLARE. It's still possible.

KATE. There is no gum in here.
CLARE. Look in my locker.

(CHARLENE enters. She is in her early thirties. She is full of flair. Very attractive and right out of the beauty parlor...hair, nails...the works. She wears an expensive fur coat.)

CHARLENE. Hello, girls.
KATE. Oh, say...look at you.
CLARE. Charlene...that coat. What happened?
CHARLENE. *(to KATE)* Guess who's comin' in today?
KATE. Mr. Taliafero.
CHARLENE. No ... I mean, guess who's comin' in ta see you? One of your favorite customers.
KATE. Sits alone, I bet.

(CHARLENE nods.)

KATE. Perfect Manhattans straight up? It figures. Shit.
CLARE. I don't know, Charlene ... some people have all the luck.
KATE. I suppose he asked for me?
CHARLENE. Who else?
KATE. Oh, great. Thanks a lot. Do you know what he does every time I start to tell a joke? Walks away before the punch line. Doesn't matter if he's sitting down at the time. He doesn't want to hear me say anything dirty. Doesn't want to know I'm human. I'm left hanging. So I turn to whoever's eavesdropping and finish it off. By that time he's clear on the other side of the dining room talking to whoever's there to save him. Weird. I want to thank you

girls for turning him over to me.

CHARLENE. Well, it was time he moved on.

CLARE. Yeah. We talked it over. Thought about it really hard. We figured you were just his type.

KATE. I told him. I said, 'Some girls have big tits ... I tell jokes. We all have to earn a living.' He cleared his throat, blushed and asked for another round. Right then I thought, 'You poor man ...'

CLARE. Poor man, my ass. He probably jerks off in his closet down on Wall Street.

KATE. You think so?

CLARE. I don't know. I shouldn't say that.

CHARLENE. He rides a bike.

KATE. Do you know what one of the night girls told me? When he comes in at night all he does is stand by the piano and sing Gilbert and Sullivan. Can't you just see it? Everyone drinking and yelling and he's singing 'I Am The Captain Of The Pinafore?' Betsy says the whole room goes into shock. One night someone said, 'Show us your tits' and he just went on...like nothing happened. Jimmy says if it weren't for the fact that he always comes in alone he'd kick him out and fuck the tips. It's that bad. I should give him to Vicky.

(CHARLENE and CLARE laugh.)

KATE. I know... I'll tell her every time I have to set up her station that she has to wait on Mr. Ince. *(to CLARE)* You can tell her it's a union rule, or something. She'll believe you.

CHARLENE. Yeah...until she goes to Stefan. 'Do I have to

wait on Mr. Ince? I can't. My nerves...what about what my doctor said?

KATE. What did your doctor say?

CHARLENE. He said I have a nervous condition. I can only wait on big tippers. And I said, "Could you make out a prescription? I have to tell my boss."

KATE. You mean, "I have to tell Rhonda," would be more like it. What is it with the two of them anyway?

CHARLENE. Don't ask.

KATE. I know about the Mafia, for heaven's sake. It's not as if I'm naive. I've been exposed - maybe not like those two - but you know what you're talking about, right?

CHARLENE. Let's just drop it.

KATE. What about what happened to your husband? That was the real thing, wasn't it?

CHARLENE. Kate.

KATE. Well, shit, why does everybody get to have a past and I don't?

CHARLENE. Don't ask.

KATE. Will guns come out of the walls?

CLARE. You want a jelly bean?

KATE. You know something? I bet if you told Vicky off, just once---really did a beauty---she'd shut up.

CLARE. Who knows?

KATE. Why not? Just tell her what you really think of her.

CLARE. I don't know---I keep hoping there's a better way.

CHARLENE. You really do belong in the mountains--- you're head's in the goddamn clouds.

CLARE. Thanks. I thought you were on my side.

CHARLENE. *(to CLARE)* How can you eat jelly beans first thing in the morning?

CLARE. I'm still here from last night. I never leave this place, don't you know that? I just smile and serve; smile and serve.

(We hear a toilet flush.)

CLARE. I don't even know what my eyes are looking at anymore.

CHARLENE. Don't you think you ought to take it easy for a while?

CLARE. What for? It wouldn't make any difference.

CHARLENE. How d'ya know? Ya haven't tried.

CLARE. I've tried. Ugh, I'm getting fat!

CHARLENE. Ya been workin steady---days and nights for close ta two months now, am I right? Ya gotta quit drivin yourself so hard. It's only gonna make things worse.

CLARE. Don't say that. I'll get depressed.

CHARLENE. Well, if ya kill yourself what good'll it do ya? You're goin about it all wrong.

KATE. Boy, you can say that again. That's the story of my life. You wouldn't like to be late girl for me, would you?

CHARLENE. I can't.

CLARE. Did something happen?

CHARLENE. I'll tell ya later. We'll go for a quick drink after lunch.

CLARE. I can't. I'm first girl. I'm already on the schedule. Come on...Kate's alright.

KATE. Yeah. You know, it isn't good to keep secrets...not from your friends, anyway. You hold all that energy in your body and it distorts your muscles. Think of your beauty. It's at stake.

CHARLENE. Where do you get your facts? *Believe It Or Not?*

KATE. It's the truth. I don't remember where I read it, but I know I did.

CHARLENE. I don't know.

KATE. You don't know what?

CHARLENE. About you.

KATE. What about me? We were talking about you. What you did last night and where did you get that coat? *(to CLARE)* Isn't that what you wanted to know?

CHARLENE. Kate, you talk too much.

KATE. I haven't said a word. Not one word. I was just teasing. I mean everything is always such a big secret. Just once I'd like you to come in here and say, "Guess what I did last night?"...at the top of your lungs...with all the girls standing here. I'd still be interested.

CHARLENE. You're too much.

KATE. Well, I would be.

CHARLENE. Good for you.

(KATE and CHARLENE begin to put on their costumes. DANUSHA is still in the john. CLARE is in the bathroom trying to put on a wig.)

KATE. Where are my stockings? Those fucking night girls think they can just help themselves. Why is it always my locker. I'd like to know? - Primadonnas.

(The girls continue dressing in silence. Then:)

DANUSHA. *(from the john)* Aaaaaooooouuuuummmm.

(No one reacts.)

KATE. I have this fantasy. On my last day here when Mr. Ince comes in and orders his perfect Manhattan straight up with a twist... I'm going to serve it to him with great innocence, as usual. I'll bat my eyes and ask him how's his seat on the stock exchange; Gilbert and Sullivan; his mother ... you know, the usual. And when he's said, 'Fine, fine, fine' about a hundred times with his funny little mouth, I'll look deep into his eyes, smile sweetly and say, 'Mr. Ince? Fuck.' Then I'll turn around to the entire dining room and say, 'I'm a woman of the world, you assholes. I'm a human being. A human woman person. What do I have to do to make you understand?'

CHARLENE. You don't think we could skip this this morning, do you?

KATE. I've got to get out of here.

CHARLENE. We all gotta do that.

KATE. No, I mean this afternoon. I know I'm right for that part. My time has come. I feel it in my bones. *(She looks at herself in the mirror. She is half dressed.)* "Give me that writing. They told me you were fools. You promised me my life, but you lied."

(CHARLENE shakes her head in disbelief.)

KATE. *(to CHARLENE)* Don't you want to know what happens?

CLARE. *(from the bathroom)* Goddamn it.

CHARLENE. What's the matter?

CLARE. Oh, nothing. I hate my face. You know, same old hum drum thing.

(CHARLENE enters the bathroom and looks uncertainly at CLARE'S wig.)

CLARE. I thought this would help.

CHARLENE. You? Miss Au Natural.

CLARE. Yeah...me. Okay?

CHARLENE. Well, I think ya got it on backwards.

CLARE. Oh. Well, a curl's a curl...know what I mean? How's this?

CHARLENE. Ya look like a million bucks.

CLARE. "Oh, honey...you're just saying that."

CHARLENE. Damn right. *(She takes the wig and looks at the label.)*

CLARE. It's a good wig.

CHARLENE. I didn't say nothin.

CLARE. I thought you'd approve. *(She takes her wig back and puts it on.)* I could've gone to Korvette's and gotten one of those shiny nylon things...they're a lot cheaper.

CHARLENE. Yeah, and ya coulda had your hair styled while you was at it.

CLARE. That's not too bad, is it? Say it's not too bad.

CHARLENE. It's not too bad. It makes ya look...I don't know...more...

CLARE. With it? Maybe?

CHARLENE. Sure. Ya just need some lashes is all.

CLARE. I don't like lashes.

CHARLENE. I know ya don't...but like I tell ya, they bring out your eyes.

CLARE. So, who's looking?

CHARLENE. Never mind about that. Just do it for yourself. He'll come around like I told ya.

CLARE. But Charlene, nothing works. I even quit wearing T-shirts to bed like you said. I don't think he even noticed.

CHARLENE. Well, he would've if youda bought the nightgown I picked out instead of that flannel thing.

CLARE. I looked dumb and you know it.

CHARLENE. No dumber than ya look in your costume.

CLARE. Well, I look dumb in my costume.

CHARLENE. Will ya quit it? D'ya think Gus woulda hired ya if ya did?

CLARE. Sure. He doesn't care how we look as long as we can carry heavy trays. Why do you think if you work out days he never promotes you to nights? Not that I mind--- cocktails can get pretty boring and I don't sing...and some of those girls...whew...not too much upstairs. Anyway all of this...it's not the same as the nightgown.

CHARLENE. It is so. Ya ain't never stopped ta think of yourself as sexy. You're always somethin else---too fat or too strong, or too ugly or your hair ain't right. Ya got beautiful hair, if you'd only set it.

CLARE. (Takes off her wig.) It was a dumb idea, wasn't it?

CHARLENE. Will ya give yourself a chance? Ya never give yourself a chance. (Takes the wig and starts to brush it out.)

CLARE. He didn't come home last night.

CHARLENE. Oh, honey.

CLARE. Didn't even call.

CHARLENE. Don't say that.

CLARE. It's the truth. He hasn't done that in a long time. Not since the group broke up. He's always at least called.

CHARLENE. I tell ya...if it isn't one thing it's another. Don't you think it's time you said something to "Our Friend"?

CLARE. Oh... We don't know anything, not really, not for sure.

CHARLENE. Aren't ya up ta here?

CLARE. Yes.

CHARLENE. Why d'ya take it?

CLARE. What can I do? Everything I try is wrong.

CHARLENE. Maybe it's time ya started fightin fire with fire.. know what I mean?

CLARE. Have an affair?

CHARLENE. Why not? It'll make kim think twice. It always does.

CLARE. Yeah.

CHARLENE. Listen, if it's meetin guys you're worried about, the Rolls Royce knows plenty---and they ain't all married or in advertisin', neither. We could double date. Ever think of that?

CLARE. Oh, Charlene...all I want to do is go back to Colorado like we planned. I don't want to have an affair. I couldn't do it. It's nothing personal...but I couldn't do it. I'm sorry. I don't mean to get upset. I really don't. I promise. I don't know what's the matter with me.

(KATE senses she's missing something and finds her way into the bathroom to comfort CLARE. DANUSHA wanders in from the john and stares at herself in the mirror...looking for something that isn't there. CLARE sees KATE.)

KATE. Is it your husband?

CLARE. Oh, well...oh...never mind.

CHARLENE. Honey, it's everything.

CLARE. Let's just drop it. *(to CHARLENE)* I'm just not like you that way, I guess. I'd rather be in the kitchen. Maybe I'm crazy, but I like it there. All this other business...I can't pull it off. I don't know...I should've been a pioneer. I guess I was just born too late.

CHARLENE. Now, I'm tired of hearin you talk like that.

CLARE. Oh, I only do it to get a rise out of you.

CHARLENE. I wish I could cook as good as you. I wouldn't have half my problems, know that? I still have dreams about your carrot cake. And so does the baby.

KATE. So do I, for that matter. Besides, what is it they always say? The way to a man's heart is through his...

(CLARE lets out a low moan.)

KATE. Did I say something wrong?

CLARE. No. No, no, no, no---no, no, no.

KATE. You're just feeling sorry for yourself.

CLARE. That's right, I am. I am. But I do it so well.

KATE. He loves your cooking and you know it.

CLARE. Well, he used to...that's for sure. He used to be very proud of me.

KATE. So he probably still is...only he doesn't know how to tell you.

CLARE. Well, all he's got to do is open up his mouth and make noise. What's so hard about that? I'll get the message. It used to be when I'd get an idea for something that he couldn't wait until I made it. He'd call up all his friends and invite them over for dinner. Everyone got to write down his opinion in my cookbook. That's how we got the idea for the restaurant. It's right in there, under pecan pie.

KATE. Do you know what she's talking about?

CHARLENE. Search me.

KATE. What restaurant?

CLARE. You guys can go fly yourselves.

KATE. Oh, wait a minute...how could I forget? You mean this restaurant, right? *(Picks up the recipe book.)* Charlene, I think I've figured it out. She's talking about the farmhouse. The one in Colorado. The one they're going to convert?

CLARE. In your ear.

KATE. You know...the one that's going to solve all their problems? He can start writing again and she can cook.

CLARE. Up yours.

KATE. Touchy, touchy. *(to CHARLENE)* These are her secrets to success. Recipes...all signed, beautifully hand written and full of unbelievable longings for second helpings.

CLARE. Give it.

KATE. Gold..do you hear me? Gold.

CLARE. Give it.

KATE. Not until you say, "Clare is worthwile."

CLARE. What?

KATE. Come on---say it.

CLARE. Will you fork it over? *(Makes a move toward KATE.)*

KATE. *(Holds the cookbook upside down as if to spill it.)* Uh, uh...

CLARE. Clare is worthwhile.

KATE. Here...catch. *(She throws book and pages fall all over the floor.)* Whoops. I'm sorry. I just don't have any style.

CLARE. Sometimes, Kate...sometimes...

KATE. I know, I know.

(They pick up most of the recipes.)

KATE. You want to know the truth? I've always wanted to do that. Just give the business the finger and run off into the woods and bake bread.

CLARE. Don't kiss up to me.

KATE. No, I mean it...it's a dream of mine---for another lifetime, probably.

CLARE. What's wrong with right now?

KATE. Well, nothing...except that I'm not doing it, am I?

CHARLENE. Let's go for a drink after lunch...just a quick one.

CLARE. I told you, I can't. I don't really want to talk about it anymore, anyway.

KATE. Maybe you should.

DANUSHA. *(to the mirror)* Ah, such is so.

KATE. No, really. I mean, level with him. Say, "Why are

we having all these problems? Why can't we do what we planned?" You know, communicate. Tell the truth...or whatever it is people tell under those circumstances.

CHARLENE. Don't you have ta comb your hair?

KATE. Now, wait a minute. I'm just trying to help. Can't I help? Am I talking too much?

CLARE. No, it isn't that.

CHARLENE. Just comb your hair.

KATE. I am, aren't I? I'm sorry, Clare. I come here, I do my work and I leave. I'm trying to remember that. I never should've read "I'm Okay---You're Okay"...but it was a good book. I'll shut up now. *(Sits beside DANUSHA.)*

CHARLENE. You still want to wear this thing?

CLARE. I think I better.

CHARLENE. *(Hands CLARE her wig.)* We gotta get your own hair out of the way first. Hold on a minute.

KATE. *(to DANUSHA)* God only knows where Vicky is. I'll probably have to wait on her tables as well.

CLARE. *(to CHARLENE)* So tell me what happened to you?

CHARLENE. Well, after I left you I was feelin' so low I went ta Bloomingdale's and there he was in the revolvin' door. Speakin' of the devil, right? I got all flustered. I ran inside and headed for the lower level. Lingerie. I figured he'd never find me there. Me, Miss Super Cool. And suddenly I feel this hand on my shoulders and he's right behind me. Do you have any bobbies?

KATE. *(to DANUSHA)* If I showed you my palm could you tell me whether or not I'll get St. Joan?

DANUSHA. I can tell you whether or not you'll have the opportunity.

KATE. Well, I already had that...all I had to do was read Backstage.

CLARE. *(to CHARLENE)* Go on.

(DANUSHA takes KATE'S palm and starts to read it.)

CHARLENE. *(to CLARE)* So I says, "What do ya have ta say for yourself?" And he didn't say a word...nothin'...just puts his hand in his pocket and pulls this package outa his pocket and tries ta hand it ta me. "Shouldn't ya be on your way ta Greenwich," I says, "You're gonna get in trouble." "I was on my way ta Queens," he says...finally. Ta see me. So I take the box. I open it and it's this. *(Shows CLARE a huge ring.)*

CLARE. Jesus. That's beautiful.

DANUSHA. *(to KATE)* You have a wonderful palm. Full of adventure.

KATE. Really?

DANUSHA. In time all the right things will come to you.

KATE. What about now? What's wrong with some of the right things coming to me now?

DANUSHA. You are like the grass that grows scattered among the weeds. You have yet to go to seed before you can come up in the meadow.

CHARLENE. *(to CLARE)* So I says, "Big deal...what's this supposed ta mean, we're engaged?" Some practical joker. I can stand up for myself same as the next guy. Didn't I get my divorce? You think that was easy with him on his way ta you know where...I can think very fast when I have to. I need more bobbies.

KATE. *(to DANUSHA)* Do I get to get married?

DANUSHA. In time.

CHARLENE. *(to CLARE)* So he says, "Look, I been thinkin' it over. We can spend most of the week together ...maybe even some holidays. I'll tell her I gotta go outa town on business...and like that.

KATE. *(to DANUSHA)* What about children?

DANUSHA. Raise your life like a child.

KATE. Oh, great...I got it. Raise my life like a child. I got it. I'm a late bloomer. I've been a late bloomer all my life. I'd just like to know when I'm supposed to get down to it? I mean, probably when I'm buried I'll grow flowers and everyone will stand around saying, "See, I knew she had it in her." I'm sorry. I guess you're right. I feel so big and behind everybody. I don't want to raise my life like a child. I want to live. You wouldn't like to be *late* girl for me, would you?

DANUSHA. I can't. I've got somewhere to go.

CHARLENE. Do either of you have any bobbies?

KATE. I do. *(Goes to her locker and gets some.)*

CLARE. *(to CHARLENE)* So continue.

CHARLENE. So he says he'll tell her he's outa town like I told ya...but I shake my head 'no'...like it's not good enough. I don't want no lies. I got my kid ta think about. It's enough I gotta explain about her father to her when she grows up.

KATE. *(Goes into bathroom with bobby pins, gives to CHARLENE.)* Here.

CHARLENE. Thanks.

KATE. *(to CLARE)* What are you wearing that for? No...I mean, that looks really good. What a change.

CHARLENE. It's a good style for ya, ya know?

CLARE. So finish.

CHARLENE. So, okay. He says, "I'll set you up. I'll tell the wife. I'll lell her everything."

KATE. The Rolls Royce?

CHARLENE. Yeah, but keep your mouth shut, Kate...I don't want nobody findin' out.

KATE. It's shut...it's shut.

CHARLENE. So I says, "Look, don't make promises...I know you men. Ya wanta have your cake and ya wanta eat it, too. You'll go off next time ya get scared...when ya find out I'm not perfect. If someone don't hand ya a reason you'll think of one." 'No', he says, 'I won't...I won't. I know it.' Just like that. So I look at him...he has this look in his eyes...and I...I don't know...I believe him. Anyways, he picks up my hand...my left one...and puts the ring on my finger and says, 'We're engaged, right?' So I says, "Can the baby call you Daddy?" He smiles...like it's okay, or somethin'...then he kisses me. And we leave. On the way out I see this coat. And he buys it for me. Then we go drinkin'.

KATE. Oh, wow! I've never had an affair with a married man.

CLARE. They're no different.

CHARLENE. Maybe you should. *(to CLARE)* There. Do you have any hair spray?

CLARE. In my locker.

(CHARLENE goes to get the hair spray.

CLARE looks at herself in disgust.

KATE and DANUSHA continue dressing.

VICKY enters. She is in her early thirties. Her hair is frizzy; she wears a low-cut dress with padded shoulders -- probably from a thrift-shop. Nothing else matches -- not in style, period or color.)

VICKY. I'm sorry, I'm sorry, I'm sorry, I'm sorry. *(to CLARE)* Oh, look at you - ya gone glamorous or what?

CLARE. Kate set up your tables.

VICKY. I would've done it.

KATE. What for? I've gotten sort of used to it.

VICKY. I said I would've done it.

CLARE. You weren't here ... like you're never here.

VICKY. I couldn't help it. I had to take my kid to the hospital. I was at Bellevue. Look. *(Produces a piece of paper signed by a doctor.)* It's the truth, I swear it! Believe me.

CLARE. This is the last time, Vicky. Next time I go to the union. I don't care who your friends are.

VICKY. What's that supposed ta mean?

CLARE. Get dressed.

VICKY. But it's the truth.

(GUS knocks on the locker room door.)

GUS. *(offstage)* Are you decent?

CLARE. What do you want?

GUS. When Vicky gets here, tell her I expect her in my office. Did ya hear me?

VICKY. I had ta take my kid ta the hospital, Gus. That's why I'm late. I was at Bellevue. That's why I never showed up---it was on accounta my kid.

Gus. That's a crock and you know it!

Vicky. It's the truth, I swear it.

Gus. Charlene? Set up for five on table nineteen. Mr. Gordon.

Vicky. What's Mr. Gordon doing sitting with Charlene?

Gus. I'm expectin' you in my office after lunch. You know what it's about.

Vicky. What's Mr. Gordon doin' sittin' with Charlene? *(Opens the locker-room door. GUS has gone.)* Goddamn you.

(CLARE and VICKY exchange looks.)

Vicky. *(to CHARLENE)* What's Mr. Gordon doing sitting with you?

Charlene. That's for me to know and you to find out.

Vicky. He's my customer.

Charlene. Take him.

Vicky. You think you can come in here and hustle, don't you? Well, I've got news for you ... there is such a thing as seniority around here. Ever heard of it?

Charlene. Ya gonna go to the union?

Vicky. I might.

Charlene. Tell them *I've* been hustling? How're ya gonna prove it?

Vicky. I got my methods.

Charlene. I'm sure you do.

Vicky. What's that supposed to mean?

Charlene. Use your brain for a change.

Vicky. I use my brain.

CHARLENE. When you fuck.

VICKY. *(Goes for CHARLENE.)* Bitch.

CHARLENE. Hands off, Vicky. You got a gripe with one of the girls you go to Clare. That's a union rule ... same as no violence, Clare speaks for us.

VICKY. Oh, yeah? Since when? I make suggestions same as anyone else, don't I? She don't speak for me, do ya Clare? She speaks for you maybe ... if it's your idea. But I don't know what I'm talkin' about, right, Clare?

KATE. Why don't we start the day off with a little sisterhood? You ever heard of that? It's been around for some time now.

VICKY. Watch your step, kid.

KATE. I'm not a kid.

CHARLENE. Kate ...

VICKY. *(to CLARE)* I'm the only one who really knows what's goin' on around here. Ever think of that? I could really help you out ... give you good ideas ... but no. I never dropped out. Never milked a cow. Never lived outside of Denver. No. All's I gots two kids ta show for my life. That's all. Two kids. What's so bad about that I'd like to know? What've you got to show for yours? No kids ... that's for sure. You're too good for that.

DANUSHA. Well, I'm going to have a wonderful day today. I'm going to meet lots of interesting people ...

VICKY. You're fuckin' nuts, you know that?

CHARLENE. Quit pickin' on her.

CLARE. Get dressed.

VICKY. That's right. Change the subject. You ain't done shit for us but look the other way and you know it.

CLARE. Whatever you say, Vicky.

VICKY. Oh, right. Agree with me. Rise above it. Maybe if ya go high enough ya can pretend I'm not even here. Ain't that it? Ya know what your problem is? You're too busy pretendin'. Shit. I seen what ya wear ta work. Ya dress like a fuckin' man. I ain't never seen ya in nothin' but them boots and that puffy jacket. What d'ya want? Muscles? What title you defendin'? Huh? What title? Ya don't fool me.

CLARE. Oh, God...I give up.

VICKY. Yeah, well, you would.

CLARE. I'll tell you this now and I'll tell you this for the last time: when a customer, regular or otherwise, asks to sit with another girl...that's his business. If you think she's been soliciting then you come to me with eviden-ce...proof...such as catching them in the act, a note passed between them. Then I will go to the union on your behalf. Have I made myself clear this time?

DANUSHA. You know, we never see the sunlight.

VICKY. Where do you live?

KATE. None of your business.

CLARE. Vicky...you're late girl.

KATE. Really?

CHARLENE. Let's go.

(CLARE, CHARLENE and KATE start to exit.)

VICKY. Clare, wait.

KATE. No ... sorry. It's a new rule ... last one in is late girl ... and if you're late on the floor you get Ince.

VICKY. Clare ... you can't do this to me. My kid. I can't stay. She's really in the hospital. Goddamn, son of a bitch.

Cocksucker. Oh, fuck. *(Slams the door shut.)*

(DANUSHA throws some glitter in her hair and starts to leave.)

VICKY. You wouldn't like to be late girl for me, would you? I'll give you five.

DANUSHA. I've got somewhere to go.

VICKY. Oh, la di da. So do I. Ever think of that?

(DANUSHA sits on the bench and puts her head between her knees.)

VICKY. What's the matter? You sick?

(DANUSHA runs into the john and throws up.)

VICKY. You alright? *(Starts to undress.)*

(Toilet flushes. DANUSHA emerges after a few beats.)

DANUSHA. I'm fine.

VICKY. You got morning sickness.

DANUSHA. I'm fine, thank you. *(She sits on the bench ... still a little dizzy.)* I'm just fine.

VICKY. Will you work for me this afternoon? I really need your help.

(DANUSHA stares at VICKY.)

VICKY. Here. *(Hands her a ten.)*

(DANUSHA lets it fall to the floor.)

VICKY. Hey ... it's a ten.

DANUSHA. Keep it. *(She exits.)*

VICKY. *(Picks up her money.)* Suit yourself. *(She is left alone on stage. She stuffs the ten back into her bag and rummages through it for a cigarette and a dime. She can't find her cigarettes but keeps trying as she puts a dime in the pay-phone and makes a call. There is no answer. She slams down the receiver.)* Shit. *(She begins to take out her frustrations out on her bag ... digging further into it and muttering to herself ... throwing its contents around the locker room.)*

(RHONDA enters. She is about 20, very tall and freaky looking -- an over-the-hill groupie. She wears rolled up jeans, flashy knee socks, platform shoes and black lipstick. She is the cigarette girl and carries boxes of cigarettes; her cape and a bag.)

VICKY. Boy, am I glad ta see you. I need some cigarettes. Trues.

RHONDA. Ya got seventy five cents?

VICKY. *(still rummaging)* I got a dime ... and three, no ... four pennies. Can I give it to ya later?

RHONDA. Hey, man—how many times do I gotta tell ya, later ain't now, know what I mean?

VICKY. Don't I always pay you back? Don't I?

RHONDA. No. Ya wanta know the truth? Ya don't. I always say forget it and ya do.

VICKY. I don't either. What about the time I tipped the wardrobe mistress for you? Didn't we agree that was for cigarettes?

RHONDA. Hey—come on ... that was once in a hundred times and you know it.

VICKY. Are you callin' me a liar?

RHONDA. No, man ... just forgetful, okay?

VICKY. Jesus. Come on, Rhonda ... just this once. I'll pay you back. I promise.

RHONDA. *(Throws a pack of Trues at VICKY.)* I don't know what I listen to ya for. I guess I'm just a soft touch.

VICKY. I'm gonna pay ya back, I swear.

RHONDA. Forget it.

VICKY. I won't forget it. I'm gonna pay ya back. I got my pride, you know.

RHONDA. Yeah, yeah. *(She notices the hole in the wall.)*

VICKY. What's wrong with everyone in this shit hole? Jesus Pesus. *(Lights her cigarette.)* I come in here this morning and the first thing I find out is Gordon's sittin' with Charlene. How long d'ya figure he's been sittin' with me? A year, right? Right? Maybe longer. Anyways, ever since I got here. He's my customer. Always has been.

RHONDA. I don't know what ya mess with Gordon for.

VICKY. I don't mess with no one. Not like you think. Gordon is my friend.

RHONDA. Oh, that's right...you're cleanin' up your act.

VICKY. Don't get fresh. I got my kids ta think about.

RHONDA. The little TV stars?

VICKY. Ya wanta make somethin' of it?

RHONDA. How many times do I gotta tell ya what happened ta Betsy?

VICKY. Betsy's a cream puff and her kids is ugly. They

couldn't sell nothin'. My kids got big teeth and freckles...that's all it takes. Gordon says so and he oughta know...he owns the fuckin' agency.

RHONDA. Shit.

VICKY. They ain't gonna be no waitresses, see? If that's all I can knock into 'em. They ain't gonna be no waitresses nor nothin' else. I'm gonna get their pictures took. Soon as I get the money, Gordon wouldn't steer me wrong. He's not that kind of guy.

(RHONDA takes a can of hairspray out of CLARE'S locker and stands on a chair.)

KATE. *(offstage)* Vicky, you got a table.

VICKY. Oh, fuck...I'm comin', I'm comin'. On top of everything else I'm stuck downstairs next to the Mouth. It's Friday. It's gonna be dead til one o'fuckin' clock and she's gonna be crackin' her goddamn jokes. She's got a screw loose, I tell ya. She tries out her jokes on any of my tables, I'll break her neck...All American Cunt.

RHONDA. Save your breath. She's a kid.

VICKY. Look who's talkin'. She's got four years on you easy. Don't get cocky.

RHONDA. Four years of what? Boarding school, college---goin home for Christmas? Where's that at? I had four years on her before I was even born...four years of experience. Like I said...she's a kid.

KATE. *(offstage)* Vicky!

(RHONDA sprays hairspray into the hole in the wall.)

VICKY. I'm comin', for Christ sake.

(Swearing in Greek is heard on the other side of the wall.)

RHONDA. *(laughing)* Why don't you try gettin' it at home for a change?

VICKY. Cocksucker.

KATE. *(Enters.)* I'm not coming downstairs again. Next time I'll take the order and the table. Stefan said I could.

VICKY. Will you listen to her? Miss Twitchit.

(More cursing is heard from other side of wall.

RHONDA. *(to the wall)* Pervert.

KATE. Don't you think someone ought to go to Gus about that?

RHONDA. Be my guest.

VICKY. Oh, shit.

KATE. *(to VICKY)* I hope you heard what I said ... because I meant it. I may appear to be all over the place but there is great order to my thinking process ... when you think about it. Are you coming or do I take the table?

(A knock is heard on the locker room door. It opens slowly. EDIE enters ... timidly.)

EDIE. Excuse me ... I'm looking for the manager ... Mr. Gus Minetti?

RHONDA. You just missed him. He's probably in the men's room washing out his eye.

KATE. Gus?

RHONDA. Well, it wasn't Daddy Warbucks.

VICKY. What do ya want him for?

EDIE. I got a call a little while ago...about a job.

RHONDA. Vicky, show the nice girl where to go.

VICKY. Show her yourself.

RHONDA. Oh...heavy.

KATE. Here, I will. Is he expecting you?

EDIE. I think so.

(KATE and EDIE exit.)

VICKY. Who's she?

RHONDA. How should I know?

VICKY. Haven't ya heard anything?

RHONDA. Hey, man...I just got here. Gimme a break. You in some kinda trouble with Gus?

VICKY. She looks like nights, don't she? Think she can sing?

RHONDA. You got a mouth...you ask her.

VICKY. What's wrong with you today? You get out on the wrong side, or in?

RHONDA. I said, you in some kinda trouble with Gus?

VICKY. Okay...I'm in trouble. Will ya find out who she is? Gus is gonna fire me.

RHONDA. You are so paranoid.

VICKY. I'm not. I'm tellin' ya...I need your help. He wants ta see me in his office after lunch.

RHONDA. Hey, man...I'm tired of gettin' you off the hook around here. What's in it for me? Know what I mean? I been nice too long.

VICKY. Nice?

RHONDA. Yeah, and the Silver Bullet thinks so, too.

VICKY. What's he gotta do with this?

RHONDA. I can't keep makin' excuses for ya. It's lookin' bad and I'm the one's gettin' the blame.

VICKY. You was supposed ta explain we had a misunderstandin'. Let him down easy.

RHONDA. I wasn't supposed ta do nothin'.

VICKY. I thought you was my friend.

RHONDA. I am, so what?

VICKY. Well, I ain't no freak. I already told ya. I don't do group shit and I ain't a user.

RHONDA. Far out. Ya got integrity. That's great. Kinda kinky.

VICKY. I don't work for no man and I ain't gettin' started. Soon as I get my kid's pictures took I'm quittin' the whole business. I got more important things ta think about.

RHONDA. Ya shoulda explained that ta the Silver Bullet in the first place.

VICKY. How could I? He don't speak ta me in English ...you know that. Just a coupla words here and there. Shit. I don't speak no pig Latin or Italian or whatever it is.

RHONDA. Sicilian.

VICKY. Well, I don't speak it. Why the fuck d'ya think I asked you to? Ya understand each other. I mean, I didn't want ta insult the guy. I know when I gotta be polite.

RHONDA. You were gettin' his hopes up.

VICKY. I was just makin' conversation. I mean, I ain't no dummy. I seen him lean on that bartender for what he owed him. I seen what he done ta his fingers. I know why they call him the Silver Bullet. But I never said nothin' about workin' no house in Jersey. I didn't even know he ran one.

RHONDA. *(lighting a joint)* How bad d'ya want me ta go ta Gus?

VICKY. Who's side are you on, anyway?

RHONDA. Hey, man...you scratch my back...I scratch yours. Want some? As a final farewell gift?

VICKY. You oughta lay offa that stuff.

RHONDA. I oughta lay on it. Go ta bed in it. Take a bath in it. Sniff it for breakfast. Oh, did we get into some shit last night. Greg and this group of his came over. We did some coke...and you know how it is...one thing leads to another. This time I got me a piano player for sure. Got him wrapped around this. *(Holds up her middle finger.)* Hey, no...I'm bein' crude. Save it for later.

VICKY. You ain't goin back ta Vegas with no rock group and you know it.

RHONDA. Sure I am...and I'm leavin' you in charge. I got my orders.

EDIE. *(Enters.)* Excuse me...which one is Chrystal's locker?

RHONDA. That one.

VICKY. Shit.

EDIE. Thanks.

RHONDA. You bein' put on the schedule?

EDIE. I don't know. Mr. Minetti wants to see how I look in a costume and then he might let me follow some- body around.

VICKY. Days?

EDIE. Huh?

VICKY. Days. Lunches ... whaaaat?

EDIE. I think so. I told him I dance. I'd heard about the Gay Nineties Room -- but he said I'd have to work my way up like everyone else. Have you ever worked nights?

VICKY. Sure.

EDIE. Is it fun?

VICKY. It's a ball.

(The pay-phone rings. VICKY answers it.

> *EDIE starts to get dressed. Her false fingernails get caught in her opera hose as she tries to put them on. She panics silently...hoping no one will notice.)*

VICKY. *(into the phone)* Yeah? This phone's off-limits after twelve. What d'ya want? You already said that. Now it just so happens that I gotta go upstairs anyways -- so I'll get her. But rules is rules. Remember that for next time. Today is just your lucky day. *(Lets the receiver dangle.)* Bunch of jokers ... *(She exits.)*

> *(EDIE continues struggling. RHONDA watches the dangling phone; relights her joint.)*

RHONDA. Hey, man---don't say nothin', okay? Pretend like it's a Camel. *(She exhales and goes to pick up the receiver.)*

> *(CLARE enters. Rhonda puts out her joint and watches CLARE carefully.)*

CLARE. Hello? Oh, hi. *(pause)* You're home. *(pause)*
How are you? *(pause)* Where were you? Oh. Oh. Oh, they
are? What for? I just asked, alright? I didn't imply anything...let's not start...Alright, it was a stupid question.
I'm sorry I asked. Greg...you're being paranoid. You're
not too old. Greg...don't yell, please. Please... *(Holds the
receiver away from her ear and listens.)* I'm going to hang...
(She listens some more.) I'm sorry. I'm tired...I wasn't thinking. No, I don't...you're right. I know. I know. *(pause)* It's
just that...I don't know. It's been so long since we've been
friendly. I'm sorry. Nothing. I just want to have a good
laugh. Like we used to. *(pause)* Greg? Just tell me what you
want me to do and I'll do it. *(There is a long pause. Greg hangs
up. CLARE hangs up the receiver and leans against the pay-phone.)*
Damn you.

*(RHONDA exits slowly. EDIE gives up in frustration and rips off
    her false fingernails...trying to hide the fact from CLARE)*

CLARE. Oh, something...something.

END OF ACT I

ACT II

The kitchen. The CHEF and his assistant, HENRI stand behind the kitchen counter, downstage center, with their backs to the audience. A big black stove, pots, pans, an assortment of knives and plates of food are their territory. Downstage right is the dishwashing area and the stairs that go down to the locker room. Stage right is the door to the fire escape. Downstage left is the door to Gus' office. Upstage center are two swing doors leading into the dining room. The right door is used for entrances. The left door is used for exits except when the characters don't.

Lunch has begun to be ordered. Throughout the act, the pace will increase.

HENRI takes a swig of cooking sherry when the CHEF isn't looking. Throughout the act he will be getting drunk.

DANUSHA enters slowly from the dining room. She steps up to the kitchen counter.

38

DANUSHA. Ordering: one chop steak, medium; one filet mignon, rare; one lobster bisque.

CHEF. No. You order backwards. How many times do I tell you ... you order the appetizer first.

DANUSHA. But he wants soup as a main course.

CHEF. You order it first.

DANUSHA. I'm sorry. I wasn't thinking.

CHEF. You are always sorry. You are never thinking ... but you never change.

DANUSHA. And you are the victim of your opinion.

(CHARLENE enters from the dining room. DANUSHA writes out her order on a slip of paper.)

CHARLENE. Chef, ordering: two chop steak, one cheese omelet and one breast of chicken.

CHEF. Let me show you Breast of Chicken. *(He reaches for CHARLENE'S breasts, misses and grabs hold of her arm.)*

(DANUSHA exits into the dining room.)

CHARLENE. You know, Chef ... you work too hard.

CHEF. You are my beauty rose. Where are you born?

CHARLENE. Jersey.

CHEF. My Jersey Rose. Would you like that? I can show you better than any of those guys out there, you know?

(CHARLENE doesn't respond.)

CHEF. Come with me and I will show you how to make soup.

(CHARLENE stares at him ... used to the routine.)

CHEF. How come you don't push the special?

CHARLENE. What is it?

CHEF. Quenelle of Pike.

CHARLENE. Well, if you'll quit slobberin' on my hand I'll see what I can do about it.

CHEF. *(Lets her go.)* Little cauliflower.

CHARLENE. Whatever you say.

KATE. *(Enters from the dining room.)* Ordering: One onion soup ... extra cheese. Guess who's here?

CHARLENE. Alone?

KATE. No, with Gilbert and Sullivan. Can I pick up?

CHEF. Une minute. I don't rush. What else?

KATE. I don't know ... that's just it. He wants to see. It's for Ince, you know. I just thought if I could get him his soup he'd see a little sooner, that's all.

(JESUS, a bus boy, enters from the dining room for bread and butter set ups. He sees KATE and CHARLENE and starts making kissing noises.)

KATE. Jesus, that's gross. How many times do I have to tell you? Don't do that. It gives the wrong impression --- It's been done before, know what I mean?

JESUS. Sos loca, sabe? Te patine el coco. You head ice skates.

KATE. Well, yours would too if you had people kissing and sucking at you all day long.

JESUS. Ay, mami...tell me, tell me.

KATE. Oh, stop it, will you?

(JESUS hands KATE a piece of paper.)

KATE. Who's this for?

JESUS. Mr. Tittman.

KATE. A club soda and lemon?

JESUS. That's what he say. He ride the wagon.

KATE. He's on the wagon.

JESUS. In the wagon.

KATE. *(to CHARLENE)* How much do you want to bet there's a full moon? How am I going to make any money? Mr. Tittman's my biggest drinker.

CHARLENE. *(to JESUS)* Is that for me?

JESUS. Si.

CHARLENE. You're a real sweetheart, ya know that? Can ya take em some water, too?

JESUS. I got. I got.

KATE. *(to CHARLENE)* Oh, great nail polish.

CHARLENE. Ya like it?

KATE. I sure do. I've always wanted long nails and long hair. I take gelatin but a lot of good it does me.

CHARLENE. It's the first time I've tried it.

KATE. Well, it's beautiful. What's it called?

CHARLENE. 'Reckless Emotion.' Jose recommended it to me a long time ago ... but I wasn't sure if I was ready for it.

KATE. Oh, yes, you are.

(The CHEF puts KATE'S soup on the counter.)

KATE. Thanks.

(CLARE enters from the dining room. KATE and CHARLENE exit. CLARE goes to the coffee machine and pours herself a cup of coffee ... the dregs. She fills the coffee machine and starts a new pot. JESUS exits. VICKY enters from the dining room ... a tray of cocktails in her hand.)

VICKY. Ordering: one sirloin steak and two chop steak ...

CHEF. You write it down.

VICKY. I can't. I got my hands full.

CHEF. You will write it down.

VICKY. Oh, fuck. Never mind ... I'll come back.

CLARE. Isn't it your turn to make coffee?

VICKY. I said I'd come back. *(Exits into the dining room.)*

CLARE. *(after her.)* You can get your own creamers. I'm not setting up your sideboard.

CHEF. Ah, Vicky. She and Rhonda ... they are two, uh, how you say?

CLARE. Two of a kind. *(She makes coffee.)*

CHEF. What's the matter with you? You are grey today.

CLARE. Oh, it's nothing.

CHEF. You work too hard. Come on. You smile for Chef. You want me to give you the secret to make the bread rise?

CLARE. You already gave it to me. A little ginger and a little sugar.

CHEF. Ah, well, then ... you know all there is to know.

CLARE. Yeah, right. That's why I'm grey.

(CHARLENE enters from the dining room. The CHEF exits to get food from the locker. HENRI takes a swig of sherry.)

CHARLENE. *(to CLARE)* Oh, there you are. Do you remember Mr. Taliafero's key number?

CLARE. N6197.

CHARLENE. What about his address?

CLARE. 400 Park.

CHARLENE. You'd think I'd know it by now. I guess I've got a block against it... don't know why. Mr. Gordon wanted to know who the new girl was -- he didn't even recognize you. I says, "That's no new girl ... that's Clare. Don't she look good with curly hair?"

CLARE. Yeah ... fat chance.

CHARLENE. He says, "Yeah, real cute."

CLARE. Well, he had to say that, didn't he? I mean ... well, he knows we're friends.

CHARLENE. You alright?

CLARE. Yeah. *(Averts her eyes.)*

CHARLENE. You sure?

CLARE. He called.

CHARLENE. Well?

CLARE. He said he spent the night at Johnny's. The group's thinking of getting back together behind a new girl.

CHARLENE. Did he say who?

CLARE. No. I didn't dare ask. Charlene? I never gave him the number of the pay-phone downstairs.

CHARLENE. Did she?

CLARE. I don't know. Isn't that something?

CHARLENE. Don't ya think ya oughta find out?

CLARE. What for? It was all my idea in the first place. I put the sign on the bulletin board.

CHARLENE. Honey, that was for voice coachin' lessons for the girls and so's he'd have a job. Ya didn't do nothin' wrong. Ya gotta start stickin' up for yourself. Look, do you know how long you've been here?

CLARE. I don't know...three...three years.

CHARLENE. Four.

CLARE. Four?

CHARLENE. Four. That's a long time, ain't it...for the sake of some farm. Ya wanta be eighty when ya turn that place inta somethin'? Ya got plans. Why else did he quit his writin' and hook up with the group? Why else did ya come ta this dump? He made ya a promise.

CLARE. We both made it.

CHARLENE. That's my point. You're upholdin' your end. What's he been doin'? Messin' around with some group and gettin' high.

CLARE. Well, what do you want me to do about it? Things haven't worked out like he planned...but he's not a shit. He's tried very hard. Sometimes people need time.

CHARLENE. Yeah, and sometimes you got a right ta say somethin'.

CLARE. I don't want to blow it. If I let on that I know or that I'm hurt...I'll blow it, Charlene. I'll lose my head and say things I'm sorry for. That'll be the end of everything--- the restaurant, everything...I know it. I can't talk to him. Not now. It would be a big mistake. I've got to be calm. I'm not calm.

CHARLENE. What about talkin' to Rhonda?

CLARE. What's that going to solve? He's just picking up where he left off. She's nothing special.

CHARLENE. Yeah, see...that's where you're wrong. Rhonda's somethin' very special. She enjoys what she's doing. She likes watchin' people squirm. Ta her it's like goin' ta the movies. Why if you wasn't workin' together I bet she wouldn't even give him the time of day, know that?

CLARE. That's sick.

CHARLENE. Ya don't have ta tell me.

CLARE. I never said two words to her.

CHARLENE. Well, maybe it's time ya did. Listen, right now ya gotta let Rhonda know who's boss. Next time ya bump inta her ya indicate that ya got some sort of suspicion. Say, "Hey, guess what? I decided to grow my nails."

CLARE. What?

CHARLENE. That's what she'll say...what?...just like you. So then ya say, "Think about it" ... real casual...and ya smile like "Don't fuck with me" ... and ya walk away. Will ya try that for me?

(The CHEF re-enters with hamburger. EDIE enters from Gus' office. She is radiant.)

EDIE. Guess what? I got the job. I mean, I'm supposed to start training. Gus says he wants to see you about it.

CLARE. Okay. Put your purse over there...by the counter.

(EDIE does so.)

CLARE. Better get a pan.

CHARLENE. Maybe I oughta say somethin' ta What's Her Face? Just ta sorta get things rollin'.

CLARE. No.

CHARLENE. Ya sure? I'm awful good at that sorta thing.

CLARE. What if I just slit my wrists?

CHARLENE. Will ya talk ta Rhonda like I said? First things first.

(EDIE returns.)

CHARLENE. Ya won't be sorry. Lemme know what happens and we'll take it from there, okay?

CLARE. Okay.

CHARLENE. Ya want me ta take her?

CLARE. It's okay. Just cover for me. *(to EDIE)* This is Charlene. I'll be right back. *(CLARE exits into GUS' office.)*

EDIE. Hi.

CHARLENE. Hi. What's your name?

EDIE. Edie. I'm sorry. My name is Edie. Charlene, right? I'm terrible with names, but I guess I'll have to learn not to be, won't I?

CHARLENE. I guess so.

KATE. *(Enters from the dining room.)* Ordering: Oh, Charlene...table 17 wants another round and Mr. Gordon wants an olive.

CHARLENE. Thanks. *(She exits.)*

KATE. Ordering: one sole almondine, extra lemon and don't burn the almonds.

CHEF. I never burn the almonds.

KATE. Relax, Chef. It's for Mr. Ince. I'm just repeating what he told me. I don't like it any better than you.

CHEF. Stupide. Why does he not cook them himself?

EDIE. *(to KATE)* Hi.

KATE. Hi. *(Exits into the dining room.)*

EDIE. *(to CHEF)* I'm Edie.

(HENRI takes another swig of sherry.)

CHEF. Eating...?

EDIE. No ... Edie.

CHEF. You are Cordon Bleu. I am your chef ... you take good care of me, I take good care of you. *(He grabs her arms.)* Know what I mean?

EDIE. I think so. *(to HENRI)* Hi.

CHEF. This is my nephew, Henri. Henri -- dites la quelque chose.

(HENRI ignores the CHEF.)

CHEF. He doesn't speak English. And sometimes he doesn't speak French, either. He is mad on me today ... I make him come to work. Lazy bum. Ah, but you are not to think about such things. You are too young and beautiful. You make me crazy. Here ... feel my heart. *(He thrusts EDIE'S hand onto his chest.)*

CLARE. *(Re-enters from Gus's office.)* Well, I see you met the chef. You can let go now...

CHEF. You are too much business ... all the time business. A man must relax with his sweetheart.

CLARE. Chef, can you wait a few minutes? Give the girl a chance.

CHEF. You Americans ... ah ... you do not understand flirtation. *(He releases EDIE and goes back to work.)*

CLARE. You ever wait on tables?

CHEF. I don't teach you about souffles.

CLARE. Chef, give me a break, okay? *(to EDIE)* It's okay. Did you?

EDIE. Once ... uh, in California? That's where I'm from. Laguna Beach?

CLARE. Laguna Beach?

EDIE. Yes. Something wrong?

CLARE. No. No, it's just funny. I had a good friend from there once. Jessy Martin.

EDIE. Oh. I've never heard of her. But maybe my mother has. She's a hostess at the Firebird. She hears everything.

CLARE. Well, she probably doesn't live there anymore. She was sort of a free spirit. We were always going to bum around Europe together and find ourselves.

EDIE. What happened?

CLARE. I got married.

EDIE. Wow.

CLARE. Yeah. Well, anyway, I've never been to California but I'll take your word you've waited tables.

EDIE. Not for very long though.

CLARE. Are you over eighteen? That's all that really matters.

EDIE. Yes.

CLARE. Okay. This is a check.

EDIE. Today's my Birthday.

CLARE. Oh ... congratulations. Learn how to keep your checks and everything will be easy.

EDIE. And here I am.

CLARE. So I see. Now, your checks. You can tell a lot about a girl by how she keeps them. Some girls are messy ... they hold everyone up -- especially when it gets busy. And some of them are neat, but they haven't got a system ... like Kate... And some of them are messy but they've got a system. Like Danusha. The only trouble with that is that it's hard to help her out because she's the only one who understands what she means. No ... what you want to be is neat and have a system. Organized up here. Your first priority is keeping your customer satisfied. You don't want him complaining or running out on you. Always keep on top of things ... even when you think you're not -- just keep going like you are. It isn't much different from running a house. *(Pauses for a minute.)* Okay. This is where we order and pick up all our food. Order it the way you write it down. Appetizers, then main courses.

(DANUSHA and VICKY enter from the dining room. VICKY uses the wrong door.)

DANUSHA. May I pick up?
VICKY. *(overlapping)* Ordering:
CHEF. One at a time. Pick up? Yes.

(VICKY gives EDIE the once over.)

CLARE. *(to EDIE)* Then you write your order on a slip of paper and hang it on my hook ... right here ... until you get a station of your own. Get that?

EDIE. *(to VICKY)* I guess I got the job.

VICKY. Ordering: two chop steak, one rare, one medium and one sirloin.

CHEF. How?

VICKY. How what?

CHEF. How you want the sirloin?

VICKY. Medium rare. It says so right here. What's the matter? Can't you read?

CHEF. You get out of my kitchen.

VICKY. Relax, will ya? I'm not finished. Ordering: two liver, very rare.

(CLARE and EDIE move to the check holder. VICKY watches them carefully.)

CHEF. Liver. I hate liver. Pick up.

(DANUSHA exits with her order. VICKY looks toward GUS' office.)

CLARE. Once you give an order put your check over here under the table number. Blank checks are kept in your costume... This is the coffee machine. A pot must be kept going at all times. Every day another girl is in charge. Today Vicky is. That means it won't get done unless anyone but Vicky does it. I don't know where I went wrong with her -- but one mistake like that around here is enough. Keep your tips and your pen in your bra and ignore the remarks.

(DANUSHA re-enters from the dining room... tray in hand. KATE follows.)

DANUSHA. Chef, this was no potatoes.

CHEF. Why don't you say so? Now what do I do? Throw them away? You want me to waste food, don't you? This is not for free. I have a budget, you know.

CLARE. *(to EDIE)* Back here is where you stack your dirty dishes.

(CLARE and EDIE exit downstage right.)

DANUSHA. He wants a salad.

CHEF. Why don't you say so in the first place?

KATE. Can I order?

CHEF. *(to DANUSHA)* You will wait your turn.

(DANUSHA sighs and uncovers her plate of food.)

CHEF. *(Grabs it away from her.)* You want it to get cold? You are folle! *(He puts the plate in the warming oven.) (to KATE)* What do you want Petite Fraise?

KATE. You can give Danusha...

CHEF. She will wait.

KATE. *(to DANUSHA)* Sorry. *(to CHEF)* Ordering: two chop steak, one very rare, one medium well.

(CLARE and EDIE re-enter and exit into the dining room.)

CLARE. Always go in and come out by the door on the right.

CHEF. Why don't you push the special?

KATE. What is it?

CHEF. Quenelle of Pike.

KATE. Oh, el puko.

CHEF. You want me to feed you after lunch?

KATE. Yes, Chef ... but not that. I don't mean to be rude, but I hate it. It's the pits. Maybe you could feed me an omelet? Hey, I'll recommend it ... I will, I promise. I'll recommend it as highly as I can without betraying my better judgement.

CHEF. Sometimes you make no sense.

KATE. That's alright. No one does. Danusha says I'm not even supposed to be here ... it's in my palm. I'm going to seed.

CHEF. *(to DANUSHA)* Here ... no potatoes.

DANUSHA. No. I said this is not the end of the line for you. Don't settle down. Don't get involved here. You have your whole life ahead of you. Keep passing through. *(Looks deep into KATE'S eyes to be sure she's gotten the message.)*

(KATE doesn't quite know what to think.)

CHEF. You want your food to get any colder? You will return it again. Only this time I don't serve you.

(DANUSHA starts to exit ... but feels a little dizzy. She sets her tray back down on the counter.)

KATE. You alright?

DANUSHA. Cramps.

CHEF. In your brain. You are folle. You don't think.

DANUSHA. There is nothing to think about.

KATE. Yes, Chef ... come on. Once a month a girl has

the right to go crazy. It's a natural law...you have to respect it. You're a man. It's your lot in life. Sorry. *(to DANUSHA)* Who's this for?

DANUSHA. Table four. Mr. Fineman. Thanks. *(Sits on the freezer chest and puts her head between her knees.)*

(JESUS enters with a tray of dirty dishes and dumps them downstage right. KATE exits with her order. CHARLENE enters from the dining room.)

CHARLENE. Pick up: two chop steak, one cheese omelet, one breast of chicken, okay?

CHEF. Okay.

CHARLENE. Ordering for Clare: one special, YEA!, and two Wellington, one no gravy.

CHEF. Sauce, my dear ... not gravy. Pas de sauce. Gravy is for Howard Johnson. Ah, these American men ... they don't know how to eat. Their waistline is more important than their tongue. I can show you tongue.

(RHONDA floats into the kitchen as the CHEF is about to grab CHARLENE'S arm again. He straightens up. RHONDA floats downstage right. The CHEF watches.)

CHARLENE. Chef, I gotta pick up ... it's startin' to get busy, ya know?

(DANUSHA gets up off the freezer chest. She and CHARLENE exchange looks.)

DANUSHA. Cramps.

(JESUS re-enters from downstage right.)

JESUS. *(to DANUSHA)* Mr. Schwartz want you to read his hand.

DANUSHA. Thanks.

JESUS. He married and got three kids...one girl...

DANUSHA. You're not supposed to tell me.

JESUS. But he make a bet with me you don't get it right. I say, "Yes, you do...you are the best. You tell Gus his fortune alla time and you never wrong since you got here."

DANUSHA. How much did you bet?

JESUS. Five dollar.

DANUSHA. Here, take this. It's all I've got right now but I'll make it up to you.

JESUS. You crazy?

DANUSHA. I don't cheat.

JESUS. Ay, pero...what difference?

DANUSHA. You shouldn't bet. You should have faith. It's much better for you.

JESUS. *(Takes the money. He is thoroughly confused. He looks at CHARLENE and shrugs.)* You wanta go out tonight?

CHARLENE. Big spender, huh?

JESUS. Sure. I show ya the town. We go to Roseland.

CHARLENE. Maybe in a couple a years. Right now I'm too old for ya.

JESUS. You scared?

(KATE enters.)

CHARLENE. Yeah, that too.

KATE. *(to CHARLENE)* Charlene, Stefan gave me this order and Mr. Gordon wants another olive. What's with him, anyway?

CHARLENE. Thanks. Will ya watch all this for me?

KATE. Sure.

(CHARLENE exits into the dining room.)

KATE. Mr. Fineman is such a jerk...you know what he does to me? He tries to grab my ass. I turn around and glare at him and he says, "You don't know it---but you're lucky. You're so low slung you could sue the city of New York for building the sidewalk too close to your ass." Ha, ha, ha. Where do they come from, I ask you? And are they really the fathers of our country?

JESUS. Ay, carrajo.

KATE. Ay, carrajo.

JESUS. Rrrrrr...carajo.

KATE. Rrrrrrrrrr,,,

JESUS. Ca-rrrrra-jo.

KATE. Ca-rrrrra-jo. Carrrajo.

JESUS. You got it.

KATE. What's it mean? *(to HENRI)* Jesus is teaching me Spanish---maybe you could teach me French. I have a natural ear. Want to hear? *(to JESUS)* What was that word? Marry...

JESUS. Marecon.

KATE. Marecon. Pretty good, huh? I keep it up I'll be able to get a job at the UN, translating or something, right Jesus?

JESUS. Estas mas loca que una cabra.

KATE. What?

JESUS. You crazy like a sheep.

KATE. Like a sheep? ...That's the first time I've heard that one.

CHARLENE. *(Re-enters with a shot glass with an olive in it.)* Jesus, table 6 wants more water.

(JESUS exits. DANUSHA follows with her salad.)

CHARLENE. Guess who just came in?

KATE. Who?

CHARLENE. Mr. Chenowith.

KATE. Who's he?

CHARLENE. Take a look. He's real nice. Tall.

KATE. *(Opens the kitchen door and peeks out.)* Oh, yeah ... sort of like William Holden.

CHARLENE. Can I pick up?

CHEF. Une minute.

KATE. William Holden and Walter Pidgeon. Where's he from?

CHARLENE. Indiana, I think. The best kind. From outa town. He's got class. Real class.

KATE. Oh, well, that figures. Stefan's putting him on Vicky's station. Table twenty. What's she got that I don't? Will you tell me that?

CHARLENE. Nothin', honey ... take my word.

CHEF. Yes, pick up ...

CHARLENE. And ordering: one bisque, one cheese omelet -- two special.

CHEF. You are my special.

KATE. *(Returns to the counter.)* My little fish.

CHEF. Who ask your opinion?

KATE. Nobody, really. But that doesn't seem to matter. I just keep giving it away, anyway.

CHEF. Two chop steak.

KATE. It's probably an oral fixation of some sort. Not enough sex.

(RHONDA re-enters from downstage right. CHARLENE turns to leave. Their eyes meet.)

KATE. Not enough? Shit. It's a goddamn desert. Everyone I know wants to be friends.

RHONDA. *(to CHARLENE)* I think Stefan was lookin' for you. Somethin' about another round.

(CHARLENE exits.)

KATE. *(Exits and re-enters immediately.)* I forgot to pick up. One sole almondine, extra lemons.

CHEF. You want sex?

KATE. What?

CHEF. You say so.

KATE. Uh, no ... I didn't mean ... I mean, yes, I do ... I guess ... but not with just anyone, know what I mean?

CHEF. I am not just anyone. I am your chef.

KATE. Yeah, I know ... uh, look ... can I pick up? I'm in a hurry.

CHEF. You think I run this kitchen just for you? You are very fresh.

KATE. I know. But I don't mean to be ... I'm young you know. Can I have my sole?

CHEF. Taissez vous.

RHONDA. *(to CHEF)* You got anything sweet?

KATE. *(to CHEF)* Extra lemon?

CHEF. *(to RHONDA)* I don't talk to you.

KATE. *(to CHEF)* I'll buckle down, I promise.

RHONDA. *(to CHEF)* Hey, all's I wants somethin' to eat, okay?

(The CHEF gives his back to the girls.)

RHONDA. *(to CHEF)* What's the matter? You got your period?

KATE. There's a full moon, I'm telling you.

(RHONDA undoes a pack of cigarettes.)

CHEF. Not in the kitchen.

RHONDA. What? I'm just lookin' at 'em. How long and thin they are. *(She shoots a gun ... it is a cigarette lighter.)*

CHEF. You smoke outside.

RHONDA. Who's smokin'? I just like playin' with fire ... same as you.

CHEF. You get out of here or I go to Gus.

RHONDA. You're cute, you know that?

CHEF. Get out.

(RHONDA exits out the door to the fire escape, stage right.)

CHEF. *(Puts KATE'S order on the counter.)* Pick up ... extra lemons.

KATE. You burned the almonds.

CHEF. Get out.

(KATE exits into the dining room ... grumbling. EDIE and CLARE enter.)

CLARE. *(to CHEF)* Chef, you seen Rhonda?

CHEF. On the fire escape.

CLARE. *(to EDIE)* Okay, now I want you to pick up this order. What are you going to do?

EDIE. *(Takes the order off CLARE'S hook.)* I say, two Beef Wellington...

CLARE. Picking up.

EDIE. Huh?

VICKY. *(Enters in a stew.)* Ordering: one mushroom omelet, two newburg. Picking up: *(Reaches for the order on her hook.)*

CLARE. *(to EDIE)* Picking up. You've got to make it clear. Are you ordering or picking up?

VICKY. I'm picking up, for Christ's sake. Two chop steak, one sirloin medium rare.

CLARE. *(to EDIE)* Never mind. Just answer the question.

(VICKY moves to the kitchen door. She opens it and peeks into the dining room. Something is obviously going on that is disturbing her.)

EDIE. I'm picking up.

(RHONDA re-enters from the fire escape and slips into GUS' office unnoticed.)

CLARE. Then say so. Listen: picking up: two Beef Wellington and one special.

CHEF. No sauce?

CLARE. Yes, Chef. You see this mark? That means no

sauce. That's how Charlene writes it. She took this order.

CHEF. Vicky ... you want to pick up or do I serve it?

CLARE. *(to EDIE)* You learn after a while ... some things are always the same ... like a martini ... what's it always called?

CHEF. Vicky!

VICKY. I'm right here, for Christ's sake.

EDIE. *(to CLARE)* Um ...um ...

CLARE. Never mind. Set up your tray. After you call out your pick-up always set up your tray with covers and wait for the chef to fill it.

(EDIE sets up a tray. The CHEF fills it with VICKY'S order. VICKY returns and pushes EDIE out of the way.)

VICKY. Watch it.

(EDIE looks confused. She thinks it's her order. CLARE gives VICKY a dirty look.)

VICKY. It's my order, isn't it?

CLARE. You don't make things any easier when you shove people around.

VICKY. Who says I'm supposed to? It's my order, isn't it?

CLARE. Yes, Vicky ... it's your order.

(DANUSHA enters with a tray of dirty dishes. VICKY exits out the wrong door ... pushing past her.)

VICKY. Oh, fuck!
DANUSHA. *(to the kitchen door.)* No turtle would try to induce a frog to live this way. *(to CLARE)* Stefan wants you. Something about another round on thirteen.

(The CHEF fills CLARE'S order. DANUSHA exits behind the partition and dumps her dishes.)

CLARE. *(to EDIE)* Now take this ... no ... I'll take it. You go out on the fire escape and get Rhonda. Tell her cigarettes on eight. Thanks.

(EDIE exits onto the fire escape. JESUS re-enters from the dining room. DANUSHA re-enters and stacks her tray and covers by the counter.)

CLARE. Jesus -- Duke needs more ice in the bar.
JESUS. Ay, mami - mucho trabajo...poco dinero.
DANUSHA. Ordering: two eggs benedict, one special.
CLARE. Danusha, you got a second? We need condiments upstairs.

(DANUSHA moves slowly to get them.)

CLARE. Thanks. *(Exits into the dining room.)*

(DANUSHA leans against the counter and closes her eyes.)

EDIE. *(Re-enters from the fire escape.)* She isn't there. *(to DANUSHA)* Have you seen Rhonda? She isn't there.
DANUSHA. She isn't anywhere. She only thinks she is.

(EDIE exits into the dining room. CHARLENE and KATE enter.)

KATE. You mean just go up and say 'hello?' Isn't that a little brazen?

CHARLENE. What have you got to lose?

KATE. Well, that just seems so obvious. I mean, I've never done this sort of thing before. I'm not really experienced.

CHARLENE. Then don't say nothin'. Just give him the eye.

KATE. How? Like this? *(She makes a face.)*

CHARLENE. No. You know what I mean ... the once over. Just casual. Like you're thinkin' about what it would be like.

KATE. Charlene, you're crazy. I gotta do St. Joan this afternoon. How well do you think I'll do if I spend the entire afternoon flirting with a total stranger?

CHEF. Are you going to order or do I take a guess?

CHARLENE. *(to KATE)* How should I know? Pick up: one bisque.

KATE. Not well. Take my word ... not well.

CHARLENE. Excuses, excuses.

KATE. Alright, alright.

(DANUSHA exits with the condiments. JESUS exits with ice. RHONDA re-enters from GUS' office ... unnoticed.)

KATE. I'm ordering: one mushroom omelet, one newburg.

VICKY. *(Enters from the dining room.)* Pick up: two liver.

CHEF. Une minute. Henri, Fait l'attention!

VICKY. One more person tells me ta smile I'm gonna break his face.

(The CHEF exits to get the liver. HENRI continues drinking. RHONDA comes up behind VICKY.)

RHONDA. Hey, man...you're in deeper than I thought. Gus is real pissed. Somethin' about a no-show. I thought ya didn't work for no man.

VICKY. Am I gonna get fired?

RHONDA. No. He ain't gonna fire you. He's gonna make sure ya never work again...that's all.

VICKY. Did he say that?

RHONDA. Not in so many words. But he's thinkin' about it. Now what am I supposed ta tell the Silver Bullet when he finds out ya been workin' parties for Gus? You're gettin' me in big trouble.

VICKY. I didn't work nothin' for no one.

RHONDA. Don't jerk me around.

VICKY. I didn't.

RHONDA. Then what was ya doin' for Gus at the Americana...research?

VICKY. I was in a jam. As God is my witness. I had ta go...Gus was gonna fire me...but I never showed up. I got clear ta the door but I couldn't turn the handle. *(pause)* I couldn't turn it. Don't ya understand? I ain't no freak. I'm tellin' the truth. I ain't got it in me. I got plans. For the first time in my life I got real good plans.

RHONDA. Oh, right...pimpin' your kids on Madison Avenue.

VICKY. You shut up, you goddamn hippie freak. There's a difference. There's a goddamn difference.

CHARLENE. *(Re-enters.)* You fight outside.

VICKY. Gimme my liver.

RHONDA. Cool your jets.

VICKY. You talk ta me in English.

RHONDA. Hey, peace. We all got plans. I'm tryin' ta tell ya...the Silver Bullet could set ya up here once and forever. Look what he's done for me. With a guy like that behind ya no one can touch ya...and Gus, well, he'll kiss your ass permanent.

VICKY. I got my friends, too.

RHONDA. Like who? Gordon?

VICKY. None of your business.

RHONDA. Ain't he sittin' with Charlene these days?

VICKY. That don't mean nothin'. He'll talk ta Gus. He's done it before and he'll do it again. You ain't the only one's got pull around here.

RHONDA. It's your funeral.

VICKY. I'm outa business. And you can tell the Silver Bullet I said so.

(RHONDA starts to exit. JESUS enters and bumps into her.)

JESUS. Oh...I beg your pudding.

RHONDA. Pardon, man. Ya beg my pardon. Ya pull your puddin'. *(She exits.)*

(JESUS hands VICKY an order.)

VICKY. How the fuck am I supposed ta read this?

JESUS. Stefan say you better hurry.

VICKY. You tell Stefan ta learn how to write.

JESUS. Aye, cajones. *(Exits into the dining room.)*

(EDIE enters and approaches the counter.)

VICKY. Ordering, I hope: one onion soup, one bisque, two chop steak, medium rare.

EDIE. Ordering: two mushroom soup...

VICKY. Speak up, kid. Ya don't order with your tits, ya know.

CHEF. Pick up: two liver.

VICKY. It better be rare.

CHEF. You get out of here.

CHARLENE. *(Enters with a tray of dirty dishes.)* Vicky, ya got another round on 5 and 10 wants ta know where their food is.

VICKY. Ya wanta make somethin' of it?

CHARLENE. Sure. What did you have in mind? *(Exits behind the partition and dumps her dishes.)*

(VICKY exits into the dining room.)

EDIE. *(Waits for it to get quiet.)* Ordering: 2 mushroom soup, one onion soup, no cheese but crusts of bread would be fine as long as they don't get too soggy, three sirloin steaks, one well done, one medium rare, one very rare with no potatoes.

CHARLENE. *(Re-enters and stacks her tray and stops by the counter.)* How are ya doing?

EDIE. Fine. One cheese omelet, firm ...

CHARLENE. You can abbreviate. MR is fine for medium rare. No, don't cross it out.

EDIE. But not too brown on the outside ... how do I write that?

CHARLENE. What?

EDIE. His cheese omelet ... not too brown ...

CHARLENE. I don't know, honey ... make somethin' up.

CHEF. Come on, come on, come on ...

CHARLENE. Pick up: one cheese omelet and two special.

EDIE. And one of these ... *(She looks helplessly at CHARLENE.)*

CHARLENE. Sole Meuniere ... fish.

EDIE. One sole Meuniere ... fish.

(CLARE enters.)

CHEF. Ordering, pick up? What do you want?

CHARLENE. I wanta pick up.

CHEF. *(to EDIE)* No, you ... what do you want with my food?

(HENRI drinks.)

EDIE. Um ... I ...

CLARE. Ordering, Chef. She was ordering. Here, give me that; ordering: two mushroom soup, onion soup no cheese, three sirloin, one cheese omelet, one sole meuniere,

EDIE. I'm sorry.

CLARE. Have they finished their drinks?

EDIE. Who?

CLARE. Fourteen.

EDIE. I don't remember.

CLARE. Go take a look. Remember what I told you?

(EDIE stares at CLARE.)

CLARE. About when you could pick up the appetizer?

(EDIE exits, bewildered.)

CHARLENE. Where did he find her?

CLARE. Under a beach blanket. *(She and CHARLENE stand alone at the counter.)*

CHARLENE. *(At the counter, to CHEF.)* Ya haven't forgotten about me, have ya?

CHEF. Never, I never forget about you.

CHARLENE. Ah, Chef...you're a man after my own heart. Did ya run inta Rhonda?

(CHEF looks at bottle.)

CLARE. Have you ever felt like you're watching yourself in a movie? Suddenly I'm hearing myself say things and I don't know why. Things I've said a million times...like to the new girl. I said, "Always keep your customer satisfied." And suddenly I thought, "Why?" ... I can't explain it. I feel separated from what I mean. There's an echo.

CHARLENE. I'm tellin' ya you're workin' too hard.

CLARE. What do you suppose would happen if I really
it?

CHARLENE. Did what?

CLARE. Said, "Get it yourself...asshole." Or something
like that.

CHARLENE. He wouldn't know what hit him, that's
for sure.

CLARE. Everything would come apart at the seams,
wouldn't it?

CHARLENE. Did ya talk ta Rhonda?

CLARE. Maybe I'm having a nervous breakdown.

CHARLENE. Ya didn't, did ya?

CLARE. Not yet.

CHARLENE. Are ya gonna?

CLARE. I guess so. I don't know.

CHARLENE. Ya know, I don't mean ta be hard on ya, but
ever since we went lookin' for that nightgown ya been different. Know that? It's like my suggestions ain't good
enough for ya. Ya don't take em ta heart. I don't know
what ta do. I wanta help...but it's like ya won't let me. It's
gettin' hard ta be your friend...ya know that?

CLARE. It is?

CHARLENE. Yeah, well...sometimes. I mean, it ain't like
I ain't never had no experience.

CLARE. I know.

CHARLENE. So if ya don't want my help then just say
so.

CLARE. Oh, Charlene...it isn't that. It's not you---it's
me. Something's happening. I don't know what to make
of it.

CHARLENE. Know what I think? And this is the last time
I'll mention it. Sometimes ya just gotta go ahead...just
make a move and figure it all out later. This business with
feelin' seperate and hearin' echos...ya don't wanta think
about that stuff...it gets ya crazy. Trust me.

CLARE. You think so?

CHARLENE. Honey, I know so. Will ya try what I said?
Just try it.

CLARE. Okay.

CHEF. Alors, pick up...

CHARLENE. Thanks Chef. I'm a hundred percent behind ya. Lemme know what happens.

EDIE. *(Re-enters from the dining room.) (to CLARE)* They've
finished their drinks. Except for the man near the statue.
He's got about this much...

(CHARLENE exits with her order.)

CLARE. Okay...then you can pick up.

EDIE. Pick up: Two mushroom soup, one onion soup,
no cheese.

(HENRI drinks.)

CLARE. Learn to keep an eye out for details, like I said.
Where every-body is; whether or not they want to take
their time. Look for little ways you can improve things
while you're standing around on the floor. Ignore the
remarks, like I said. They're part of the job. You want to
work here you've got to learn to handle them. Those guys
aren't going to change. We had one girl here who thought

they might. She lasted one day. They're human, same as us. They've got their own way of making sense out of things. Know what I mean?

EDIE. Why did you come here?

CLARE. Me?

EDIE. Uh, huh.

CLARE. I wanted to learn the business and they weren't exactly putting women in tuxedos over at 21. It was the best I could do in a decent restaurant. So...where does that go?

EDIE. To the table in the corner by the palm tree.

CLARE. Fourteen. Learn your numbers as soon as you can. You're doing very well.

EDIE. I am?

(RHONDA enters from the dining room. CLARE sees her for the first time since the phone call. They stare at each other. EDIE hesitates and then leaves with her soups. DANUSHA enters with a tray of dirty dishes. She exits downstage right and dumps them. CLARE starts to say something and then stops. DANUSHA re-enters and goes to the coffee machine to start another pot. She leans on the table and rubs her stomach.)

DANUSHA. *(to CLARE)* I think one of your tables wants another round...the man with the moustache and the bread crumbs...

CLARE. You sick?

(DANUSHA starts to cough...trying to stop from heaving. RHONDA exits. DANUSHA can't make it and heads for the locker room downstage right. CLARE follows. They exit.)

KATE. *(Enters from the dining room.)* Can I pick up? Two chop steak, medium rare, medium well.

VICKY. *(Hot on KATE'S heels.)* You stay away from Chenowith.

KATE. For Christ's sake, Vicky...he just asked me to tell him a joke.

VICKY. I don't care what he asked you ... he's my customer. Stefan put him on my station.

KATE. *(to CHEF)* No peas.

CHEF. That's all I got ... peas.

VICKY. You been givin' him the eye ever since he came in here.

KATE. I have not. No, Chef ... no peas.

CHEF. Then what?

KATE. Carrots, anything.

CHEF. I got only peas. It's Friday. I got only peas. Peas only. When do you learn, you girls? You are all so dumb.

KATE. We are not.

VICKY. I catch you tryin' anything like that again I'm goin' to Gus.

KATE. What is it with you, for Christ's sake? All I wanted was a decent conversation. He's the first human being I've seen in this place, alright?

VICKY. So you admit it?

KATE. Admit what?

VICKY. That you started up with him?

KATE. I did not. He asked me to tell him a joke. Heard I had a sense of humor, I guess and wanted to be entertained, alright? Why is it such a crime to talk to someone? I don't get you, Vicky. I like a good conversation every now and then. You ought to try it sometime.

VICKY. You know what your problem is? You don't get enough. That's why you jaw so much.

KATE. I don't get any, Vicky. Isn't that great? You're right. I don't get any...but I'm working on it.

(CHARLENE enters.)

VICKY. Order...Pick up: one mushroom omlet, two newburg. I'll be right back.

KATE. What a witch.

CHARLENE. Don't let her intimidate ya.

KATE. Oh, I don't know...maybe I'm just asking for trouble. It isn't worth it.

CHARLENE. Sure it is.

CHEF. Henri, prends soin.

KATE. Yeah?

KATE. I don't know, Charlene. What if Vicky goes and tells Gus? I'll get fired.

CHARLENE. How's she gonna prove it? She's gotta catch ya in the act.

KATE. She probably will...I don't know what I'm doing.

(RHONDA enters, unnoticed.)

CHARLENE. You worry too much.

KATE. Charlene, can I ask you a question? The Rolls Royce...is he from here?

CHARLENE. That's for me to know and you ta find out.

KATE. Oh, come on...who am I going to tell? Table nineteen, right?

CHARLENE. Table nineteen. Right.

KATE. He's got great eyes.

CHARLENE. Yeah.

KATE. You're so lucky. Coming through!

(CHARLENE and KATE exit. VICKY re-enters with a drink.)

VICKY. Can I pick up?

RHONDA. *(Comes up behind VICKY.)* Oh, by the way... guess who's on nineteen?

VICKY. Gordon.

RHONDA. The Rolls Royce.

VICKY. What?

RHONDA. You heard me. The Rolls Royce. Gordon and the Rolls are one and the same. Ya still so sure ya got friends?

VICKY. How d'ya know?

RHONDA. It ain't too hard ta figure. Just keep your ears open. Come ta think of it, why's the man always ordering olives? There must be five or six shot glasses full of em and he hasn't touched a single one. You think it's love?

VICKY. How long?

RHONDA. How long's Charlene been talkin' about the Rolls? Three months, maybe?

VICKY. Who does she think she is? I'll break her neck. I don't care. I'm goin' ta Gus.

RHONDA. Hey, man...Gus ain't gonna fire Charlene. She's too connected...you know, on accounta her ex.

VICKY. What about him?

RHONDA. Never mind. You don't wanta mess with Charlene...not without some sort of protection, trust me.

VICKY. I don't care. I'm gonna kill her.

RHONDA. No, man...I'm gonna kill her and square you with Gus. I got protection, don't I?

(VICKY and RHONDA exchange looks.)

RHONDA. You scratch my back---remember? *(She exits.)*

VICKY. *(Starts to pick up her tray.)* I don't need your help. I'll think of somethin' else. *(Exits out the wrong door and bangs into EDIE.)* Will ya watch it, for Christ's sake?

EDIE. *(Stands in the kitchen in a state of shock.)* Clare? ... Clare?

(HENRI finishes the bottle.)

CHARLENE. *(Enters.)* Did ya get the rag?

EDIE. I was lookin' for Clare.

CHARLENE. Get the rag ... over there ... then go back to the bar and ask the bartender for another round of drinks.

EDIE. *(Starts to cry.)* I'm sorry. It was an accident.

CHARLENE. Don't worry about it. Get the rag. I gotta place an order. Just go tell the bartender what happened and that you need another round.

EDIE. He thinks I'm crazy.

(KATE enters from the dining room.)

CHARLENE. No, he don't. That's just the way he is. He's a nice guy when you get to know him ... wouldn't hurt a flea. He just likes ta give the new girls a hard time. We've all been through it. It's like initiation. Go tell him, okay?

EDIE. He won't give it to me, I know it.

CHARLENE. Kate, take this rag to Mr. Chenowith, will ya? Edie spilled some drinks.

KATE. To Mr. Chenowith? What about Vicky?

CHARLENE. *(Hands the rag to KATE who doesn't want to deal with it.)* What about her?

KATE. You heard what she said. She got pissed off when she saw me talking to him. Said she'd go to Gus.

CHARLENE. Will ya take the rag to Mr. Chenowith? Next thing you know I'll be teachin' ya how to kiss. Go on, will ya? Let me handle Vicky.

KATE. You mean it?

CHARLENE. I mean it.

KATE. Charlene, you are the greatest. You really are. I'm so glad I know you. *(Exits into the dining room and re-enters.)* Shit, I forgot the rag. In my hour of need, I forgot the rag. *(She exits.)*

CHARLENE. *(to EDIE)* Now go to the bar like I told you. Go on. Duke will give you your drinks. Just smile a lot. It ain't hard.

EDIE. Okay. *(Exits into the dining room.)*

CHARLENE. Ordering:

CHEF. *(Picks up the bottle of sherry, sees it's practically empty and takes off after HENRI.)* Bete. Que tu es stupide. Cochon. Animal. Sacre blue. Merde alors.

CHARLENE. Ordering:

CHEF. Minute. I am busy. Why do you not see?

(HENRI passes out.)

CHEF. *(Tries to pick him up.)* Can't you help me? What do you stand there for? If he weren't my nephew I would slit his throat like a chicken. He is a pig. *(He spits in HENRI'S face.)* Tu M'entend? Je t'envois a la France la prochain fois. Bete des betes.

CHARLENE. What should I do?

CHEF. We will lift him. There.

(They prop him up at his table—his hand under his chin.)

CHEF. Now no one will know. I will tell Gus he's thinking. Merci. Now what do you want?

(CLARE enters from the locker room, downstage right.)

CHARLENE. *(Steps up to the counter.)* Where have you been?

CLARE. Danusha's sick. She's in the locker room. I gave her the rest of the day off. We're going to have to cover. What's this?

CHARLENE. Your table 28.

CLARE. Thanks. Ordering: two special, one chop steak, rare; one mushroom omelet. Pick up for Danusha: two eggs benedict, one special. What's the matter with Henri?

CHEF. Rien. Il pense.

CHARLENE. He's thinking.

CLARE. Jesus. What's going on around here? I thought it was just me.

(VICKY swings into the kitchen from the dining room, making a bee line for Gus' office.)

CHARLENE. Where the hell do you think you're going?

VICKY. I'm going to Gus. Kate's out there hustling Chenowith.

CHARLENE. Mr. Chenowith.

VICKY. *(to CLARE)* Go ahead. Take a look. You said ya needed evidence. Well now ya got it. She's talkin' to him right now. I gave her plenty of warning, but no ... she's gone and spilled a drink in his lap. Any excuse for contact. Horny bitch. *(Goes to the kitchen door and holds it open.)* Take a look. Go on. She's doin' it right now ... wipin' up his thing.

CHEF. Ferme la porte.

VICKY. Take a look.

(The CHEF comes around to the other side of the counter.)

VICKY. *(Lets the door go.)* What's the matter? Don't ya believe me?

CHEF. You want to fight you go outside.

VICKY. You leave me alone. I'm talkin' ta Clare.

CHEF. And I tell you shut the door.

VICKY. It's shut ... It's shut.

CHEF. It's swinging ... It's swinging.

CHARLENE. Chef.

CHEF. Chef, nothing. I like my quiet and my peaces.

VICKY. *(to CLARE)* You gonna fire her or what?

CHARLENE. You wanta know who spilled that drink? The new girl. Kate was just helpin' out. I told her to.

VICKY. You stay outa this. Well? You gonna take a look or do I go ta Gus?

*(The CHEF puts up CLARE'S order. CLARE puts the covers on her
food. VICKY waits. CLARE doesn't budge.)*

VICKY. Ya think if ya stand there long enough I'll go
away, is that it? What makes her so fuckin' special, I'd like
ta know? I got rights same as the next guy. I ain't the one's
gonna get fired.

CHARLENE. Neither is Kate.

VICKY. You stay outta this.

CHARLENE. You're in trouble with Gus.

VICKY. You take a look out that door. You're fuckin'
chicken shit. Ya don't wanta know nothin'.

(CLARE picks up her tray and turns to leave.)

VICKY. *(Grabs CLARE'S wig.)* Ya wear a wig ta prove it.

CHARLENE. Give her back that wig.

VICKY. You stay away from me. *(She begins to hit
CHARLENE with the wig.)*

(EDIE enters with a tray of drinks.)

CHEF. *(Bangs his cleaver.)* Outside! Outside!

(EDIE screams. CLARE drops her tray. There is silence.)

CHEF. Ah, merde alors---mais quesque tu fais la? You
of all the peoples. I am up to here. I go to Gus.

CHARLENE. Don't ya think ya oughta wake up your
friend first?

CHEF. Alors, laisse moi. Pick up. Pick up, you clumsy.

CLARE. I'm sorry. I...I'm sorry... I don't know what got into me.

CHARLENE. It's okay.

CLARE. No, it's not. It's not okay...it's not, it's not, it's not...

VICKY. You're damned right. Jesus Christ. Ya never let me tell ya nothin'.

CHARLENE. Give her back that wig and get outa here.

VICKY. Not until she looks out that door. Go on.

CHARLENE. Boy, if you ain't the limit, I don't know what.

CLARE. Charlene...

VICKY. Why won't ya do it?

CLARE. I don't know. I don't know.

VICKY. You tell me.

CHARLENE. She already did. She don't know.

VICKY. I'm warnin' ya, I ain't takin' no more of your buttin' in.

CHARLENE. Oh, yeah? What are ya takin' these days?

CLARE. Charlene...stay out of this.

VICKY. Look, I ain't gonna hurt ya. Shit...what'd I wanta do that for? I'm just tryin' ta help. Can't I help? Ya listen ta the other girls when they got complaints---what about me? Do I got warts?

CLARE. No.

VICKY. Then tell me. I wanta understand. So's we can all be friends, okay? Here...I tell ya what...I'll even give ya your wig back...up-front..on faith. See? Take it. Go on... take it...now tell me, why won't ya look out that door?

CLARE. I...I...I don't like the way you ask me.

VICKY. You what?

CLARE. I don't like the way you ask me. When you ask for help...you...I don't like the way you do it.

VICKY. You've fuckin' gone round the bend. Are you our representative, or what?

(CLARE hesitates. Then gives up. She bends over and starts to pick up the dishes at her feet. VICKY steps on the plate she is picking up.)

VICKY. Are you or what?

CLARE. Yes.

VICKY. Then what about my rights?

CLARE. What about mine?

VICKY. What rights? You're our representative. You got your duties. You owe me.

CLARE. *(Rises.)* No, I don't. I don't owe you anything. You've done nothing but put me down ever since you got here. I don't owe you anything. If you want to think so you go right ahead but you'll never get so much as that from me until you can learn to treat me like a human being. I don't care what you think is going on on your station. Kate doesn't know the first thing about hustling and you know it.

VICKY. Look out that door!

CLARE. Don't yell at me! Don't you ever yell at me again.

VICKY. Please? Please. Please will ya look out that door?

(CLARE moves to the door. KATE has obviously gone.)

VICKY. Goddamn it. Fuck. I was tellin' the truth.

(CLARE picks up her dishes. CHARLENE has gotten a broom and starts to help her. EDIE remains frozen with her drinks.)

VICKY. Wait. Listen...I need your help. I need it. As God is my witness. Swear you'll call the union. Swear it. Just for the record...just ta register the complaint.

CLARE. I'll think about it.

VICKY. We won't have no more trouble...you'll see.

CLARE. We'll talk about it after lunch.

RHONDA. *(Enters and sees the mess on the floor.)* Oh, say... Creative Playthings.

CLARE. *(to EDIE)* You better get Duke to put some more ice in those drinks.

EDIE. Oh, no... *(Exits into the dining room.)*

RHONDA. *(to CHARLENE)* Charlene, I been lookin' for you. The Rolls Royce wants an olive. Says it's urgent. *(CHARLENE starts to go and catches herself.)* I'm sorry, who did you say? The Rolls Royce?

RHONDA. Table nineteen? Mr. Gordon?

CHARLENE. Oh, that Rolls Royce. Thank you, Rhonda. *(Exits into the dining room.)*

RHONDA. Vicky...there's a guy upstairs...wants your number. *(pause)* What are ya waitin for?

(VICKY exits into the dining room.)

CHEF. *(Puts up CLARE'S order)* Alors, pick up. Pick up.

(CLARE goes to the counter and starts to put on her wig.)

RHONDA. Here...lemme help ya.
CLARE. Uh, no...I can fix it....I've got it...

(RHONDA stands behind CLARE and adjusts her wig. She takes a comb out of her cigarette tray.)

CLARE. Thanks.
RHONDA. Don't mention it.

END OF ACT II

ACT III

The locker room. DANUSHA is lying on the bench. KATE enters.

KATE. Oh, what a day. My feet are killing me. There was a big fight in the kitchen... Clare dropped a tray of food. She got mad at Vicky. Probably for not making coffee. You know, the same old thing. Some people never learn. And Charlene is pissed at me about something ... but she won't say what, of course. Here. *(Hands DANUSHA some money.)*

DANUSHA. What's this?

KATE. Your tables.

DANUSHA. No. You keep it. I don't want it.

KATE. I'm thinking of having an affair. Just thinking about it, but don't tell, okay? Anyone in there? *(Looks toward bathroom.)* Anyway, I need a little reassurance or something. Do you read handwriting? Mr. Chenowith gave me this card. That's not getting involved, is it? Having an affair? Can I do it?

DANUSHA. I do not give you permission to run your life. You run it. You don't need handwriting analysis ... you have good instincts already. Learn about them.

KATE. But what about Mr. Chenowith? What will happen if I meet him for a drink?

DANUSHA. You want a fortune teller you go to Eighth Avenue. I am not a fortune teller.

KATE. I'm sorry. I didn't mean to insult—

DANUSHA. That's it ... we have talked enough.

KATE. But ...

DANUSHA. No buts.

KATE. Are you alright?

DANUSHA. We are all always alright.

KATE. Physically, I mean? Will you take it? The money? *(Hands her the money again.)*

DANUSHA. I didn't do half the work.

KATE. We all agreed you'd need it ... it's yours ... for your, you know -- whatever. Oh, what's the use? Clare told us ... Charlene and me ... but I don't want you to worry... you're not going to get fired or anything. Gus will never know. I'm going to take bullshit lessons from Charlene so I can answer questions without saying anything. She said she'd teach me a few catch phrases like 'That's for you to know and me to find out.' I'm going to become mysterious. Well, anyway ... we all want you to stay.

DANUSHA. *(barely audible)* Thank you.

KATE. Will you take the money?

DANUSHA. No.

KATE. *(Sets it down on the bench.)* Well, I'm putting it here. I don't want it either. You can do what you want. *(She begins to undress.)*

(CHARLENE enters. KATE takes a kleenex out of her bra and stuffs it in the hole in the wall. CHARLENE takes a dime out of her purse and puts it in the pay phone. They ignore each

other. DANUSHA begins to undress.)

KATE. I'm going to get something for lunch. Did you eat?

DANUSHA. No.

KATE. Do you want anything?

DANUSHA. Uh, that's alright.

KATE. What about some soup?

DANUSHA. I'll get it.

KATE. I'll get it, for heaven's sake ... I'm going upstairs. *(She exits.)*

CHARLENE. *(into the phone)* Hi, baby. Were you a good girl today? What did you do? Did you go high? I'm so proud of you. Can Mommy speak to Gretchen? What? I don't know, baby ... let me speak to Gretchen. *(to DANUSHA)* Who's money is that? Better not leave it lying ... *(into the phone)* Hi, honey. Is everything alright? Did she go tinkle? What about after she calmed down? Oh. Well, listen ... I've had a change of plans. I gotta work tonight -- can you go next door and ask Mrs Rugiero if she can take the baby? Tell her I'll pick her up first thing in the morning. I probably won't be back until late. Thanks.

(DANUSHA picks up the money, reluctantly, and stuffs it in her locker.)

CHARLENE. *(into the phone)* What, baby? She's going next door to speak to Mrs. Rugiero.. Not until later, sweetheart. Mommy has to work tonight. No, I didn't promise. I said 'maybe' -- but somethin's happened and Daddy can't come. Your new Daddy. Did you go tinkle in your bath water? He can't come either. Did you go tin ... what? Remember what I told you? Well, you can't have him, honey. He's gone away for a long time. Maybe until you're a big girl. Honey? Mommy's doin' what she can. Did you tinkle in the ... Don't bang the reciever. Damn it. *(She hangs up, composes herself.)* You need a doctor?

DANUSHA. No.

CHARLENE. Well, I know the name of a good one if you change your mind.

DANUSHA. Thanks.

CHARLENE. He's real nice. Personal. Better than the clinic. You want my advice you'll beat it over there.

DANUSHA. Thanks.

CHARLENE. But you suit yourself.

DANUSHA. Thanks.

KATE. *(Re-enters.)* How do you like that? The chef wouldn't give me an omelet because I returned a special during lunch. Some guy didn't like it ... he wasn't even on my station and the chef said I talked him into it. Here's your soup.

DANUSHA. Thanks.

(CHARLENE and KATE exchange looks.)

KATE. I haven't said a word. Not one word. I don't understand what you're so upset about in the first place.

CHARLENE. You and Clare are the only ones who saw the papers.

KATE. We're not the only ones.

CHARLENE. I mean that I showed that article to about my ex. Ya know his name. You know what I'm talking about.

KATE. Charlene, I didn't even know what you were talking about when you read it to me. I'd forgotten all about it because I didn't understand it in the first place. That's what I was trying to tell you. All I can think of now is exorcism.

CHARLENE. Extortion.

KATE. Well, see? At least I knew it had *exs* in it.

CHARLENE. It's got lots of *exs* in it.

KATE. It's just that I get all confused. One minute we're the best of friends and next you're on my back for something. I don't get it. Did I do something? I like you ... I really do. I consider you one of my best friends, know that? We're a team. Mr. Chenowith gave me his card.

CHARLENE. *(Bursts into tears.)* Oh, honey.

KATE. Now what?

CHARLENE. No...it's not you...it's...just the way...things ...they haven't turned out...I gotta go to work.

KATE. I thought you were going apartment hunting with the...

CHARLENE. No. We ain't goin nowhere. Don't you see? I get this message in the middle of lunch from Rhonda...the Rolls Royce wants urgent olives. So I go to him and he tells me it's off. Not in so many words...but it's off. Right in the dining room. He says, "I didn't know about your husband and his friends. I can't afford to take that kind of a chance. What about my family." How many times have I heard that? You know what he does...right before they cart him off...my ex? Throws a divorce party. I couldn't figure it out. He'd been hittin' the ceiling for two years every time I'd so much as start ta mention the subject and suddenly he's throwin' me this big party...givin' alla his friends a good look at me so's they can all keep tabs on me for the resta my life while he's in jail. You don't know how lucky you are. Ya got your whole life ta sorta grow into. But me. I had it all when I was fifteen. Looks, confidence...a sense of humor. I even had a sense of humor. I had so much. I didn't know what ta do with it.

KATE. Well, I think you've done really well. All you've got to do now is tell those Mafia creeps to mind their own business.

CHARLENE. No, honey...you don't know what you're talkin' about.

KATE. Well, then...don't.

CHARLENE. It ain't so much me as the baby. I brought her into this mess. I thought the Rolls Royce...I thought he was different...wanted to help. He could've. I didn't even want ta get married. Just the place. That would've been enough. No demands.

KATE. Yeah...

(The pay phone rings. CHARLENE answers.)

CHARLENE. *(into phone)* Hello? Yes, honey. Oh, well, you better pack her bag. I think it's over by the love seat. Yeah, give her ta me. Baby? Mrs. Rugiero's gonna take ya to her sister's for the weekend. Won't that be fun? Maybe Mommy will come and get ya on Saturday if she doesn't have ta work. Would ya like that? You can eat candy. Will ya be a good girl? Yes, honey, all ya want. I love you. Bye. Yes, a million pieces. Bye. *(She hangs up.)* I don't know how our Miss Rhonda put two and two together but I'm gonna kill her.

KATE. Maybe she didn't. Maybe she made an idle guess and was right.

CHARLENE. My life ain't the goddamn lottery!

KATE. Hey, I'm sorry.

(CHARLENE exits, slamming the door. KATE runs into the john. DANUSHA finishes her soup.)

KATE. *(from the john)* I'm going to be a star. I'm going to be a star. I'm not going to get involved with anyone. I'm going to be cold, cold, cold. Oh, if only that was true.

(DANUSHA starts to undress. CLARE enters followed by VICKY).

CLARE. I don't care. Kate sets up for you all the time. You're late on the floor; you don't do your duties...I can't just present your side. I've got to give Mr. Grasso as good an idea of who's filing the complaint as who it's against... otherwise it isn't fair. Facts are facts. *(She puts a dime in the pay phone.)*

VICKY. Listen, I was outta my head...you can forget about it, okay? It ain't Kate...she didn't mean no harm...I know that. I just wasn't thinkin' straight, know what I mean?

KATE. *(from the john)* Will someone please tell me what I did because it was probably an accident.

VICKY. It weren't nothin'. Just a misunderstandin', right? Kate ain't no hustler. I didn't know what I was doin', I swear.

CLARE. Then what do you want me to do?

VICKY. Call the union like you planned---only tell them it's Rhonda, okay? She's...she's what's behind all this, as God is my witness...may He strike me dead...I'm tellin' the truth on my children's graves, God bless them. I'm tellin' the truth.

KATE. *(emerging from the john)* Rhonda's behind a lot of things, if you ask me.

VICKY. Ya gotta help. Ya gotta. She's the one who tipped off the Rolls Royce about Charlene's ex. Don't look at me that way. It's the truth.

CLARE. How do you know?

VICKY. I just do. Ya gotta believe me...she's dangerous.

CLARE. What's in it for you?

VICKY. Nothin'. I...I just heard what ya said the other day about gettin' along and how nice it'd be if we all, ya know...really made an effort. But Rhonda's bad...she'll make it hard for us. That's how she gets her kicks. I want ta help ya.

CLARE. Then get back on the floor.

VICKY. What d'ya mean?

CLARE. You're late girl---get back on the floor.

VICKY. Yeah, but...

CLARE. When I want your help I'll ask for it.

VICKY. Charlene ain't the only one Rhonda's fuckin' with...know what I mean?

CLARE. Get back on the floor.

VICKY. Don't ya think ya oughta do somethin' or ya just gonna keep changin' the subject like always?

CLARE. I think you ought to get out of here.

VICKY. And I think you ought to know who told

Rhonda about Charlene's ex. Your husband, that's who. If youda kept your mouth shut none of this woulda happened. It's your fault. You made this whole mess.

CLARE. You get out of here.

VICKY. She's got him wrapped around this. *(Holds up her middle finger.)* She said so herself.

CLARE. Get out. Get out. Get out.

(VICKY exits, slamming the door. CLARE kicks it, grabs ahold of herself and fights for self control.)

CLARE. This is unbelievable. I never should have opened my mouth. I never should have dropped that tray. I should have served those lunches...business as usual...and just held on for dear life. What am I supposed to do?

KATE. Get angry, for Christ's sake. Only not at the door ... at Vicky. Jesus...go to Gus...something. I don't care what she said. She had no business talkin' to you like that.

CLARE. I've got to get out of here.

KATE. What do you want to do that for? You've got a chance to look the enemy in the face and...and...fight.

CLARE. What for? What good would it do to say anything? People only hear what they want to hear, don't you know that? Nothing works. Nothing ever works.

DANUSHA. Surrender.

KATE. Well, then listen...maybe you ought to go to the union like you planned only tell them the whole truth. Get it all out in the open. Say, "Look, there's a lot of creepy people where I work and a lot of nice people and if you guys aren't going to help me in my fight against creeps then I will have to take my business elsewhere. Like to Nadar's Raiders."

CLARE. Nadar's Raiders?

KATE. Yeah, you know...Ralph Nadar. Consumer's rights.

CLARE. Jesus, Kate...Jesus. Is everything a goddamn joke?

KATE. I'm serious. You're a consumer. We all are. We eat shit.

CLARE. You don't understand.

KATE. Yes, I do. That's the whole point. I do understand, that's the whole point. I mean, you and Charlene...I know you've got your own business...but it's like you only tell me half of what's going on and then I have to guess the rest. I'm not a blabber mouth. I just talk alot. There's a difference. But I do understand. I understand a lot of things---I'm a very understanding person. I know you've got problems and I know you're not just upset about Vicky.

CLARE. Well, that must have been hard to figure out.

KATE. Hey, come on...I just thought...never mind. I thought if you needed any help...maybe I could. Just,... Oh, never mind.

CLARE. I'm sorry. I know that's what you meant.

KATE. Maybe I could talk to Gus for you. Or what about the union guy? Want me to talk to him? I'll even talk to Vicky, for that matter, if you'll tell me what to say. Just tell me what to say and I'll say it.

CLARE. I don't know what to say. I don't know what to say to anyone anymore.

KATE. How about: "Vicky, you're fired." Just for starters. Consider it an experiment in the fight for human rights. What have you got to lose? She breaks the rules. Well ... she breaks the human rules. There ought to be something you can do about that.

CLARE. What? Will you tell me? What right do I have to tell anybody anything?

KATE. You're a human being, for Christ's sake. What do you think we're here for? I mean, here...not here.

CLARE. If someone could tell me that---I'd do anything for them...anything. Even wear sexy nightgowns.

KATE. Can I ask you a question?

(CLARE shrugs.)

KATE. Was Vicky telling the truth? Just now...about Rhonda and your husband? Was that the truth?

CLARE. I think so... I'm going to get some lunch. *(She starts to exit.)*

(EDIE enters.)

CLARE. Excuse me.

EDIE. I wouldn't go up there if I was you. Everyone's screaming and yelling.

KATE. That seems to be the order of the day...no pun intended.

CLARE. What happened?

EDIE. Well, the girl ... with the cigarettes? ... was walking through the kitchen and Charlene came up behind her. She was mad about a car of some sort. Maybe she didn't get a ride. Any way, the girl with the box ...

KATE. Rhonda.

EDIE. Rhonda ... said if she tried anything fancy that she'd shoot her Rolls Royce with silver bullets. Then they attacked each other. If it weren't for the Chef coming at them with his cleaver someone might've gotten hurt. It was awful serious.

CLARE. There's a full moon. I'm telling you. There's a full moon.

KATE. Well, I've been saying that all day ... but no one will listen.

EDIE. Did I do something wrong?

KATE. No ... it's complicated.

CHARLENE. *(Enters looking bedraggled.)* I gotta talk ta you.

CLARE. I know.

CHARLENE. What did you go and tell Greg for? I told you — don't tell no one about my ex — and here I been blamin' Kate.

CLARE. It never occured to me. I'm sorry. If I'd've had any idea — I'm so sorry. I never thought he'd say a word. I wasn't even sure he knew who I was talking about. Oh, Charlene. It was an accident. I was just trying to talk to him.

CHARLENE. You gotta do something. You can't just pretend like Rhonda don't exist. Not anymore. You can't. It's my life, too---ya gotta do somethin'.

CLARE. What? Will you tell me that? What? I'm sorry. So sorry. I've been sorry for so long now. How do I stop? How do I make it right? I want out. That's all. Out. How do I get out? *(pause)* I ought to quit.

CHARLENE. Don't say that. We need you around here.

Who am I gonna go drinkin' with? Kate drinks orange juice. You can't...not today. I need your help.

KATE. You've got to come to terms with the enemy before you can be free of him.

CLARE. Who is the enemy?

(CHARLENE and KATE can't answer. DANUSHA is in meditation.)

KATE. Do you have any gum?

(EDIE looks for gum in her bag. CHARLENE goes into the john and starts to fix her makeup and hair.)

KATE. Thanks. *(to EDIE)* What's in the box?

EDIE. Underwear. It's real pretty. Clare gave it to me. One size fits all. It's my birthday. She already has about twenty pairs. One of her regulars gives them to her. The man who draws on his moustache?

KATE. Did you notice that? I always thought he did but I could never tell. One day I almost asked him. But I thought I'd wait until I got some underwear. I never did. He only brings it to Clare and every now and then to Charlene.

EDIE. Maybe you're not his type.

KATE. Yeah, I know what you mean. *(Looks at herself in the mirror.)* Will you look at me? Do you believe I'm on my way to a fancy restaurant? I was going to wear boots, you know...St. Joan wears armour. Then I thought my overalls would have to do. I don't want the director thinking I'm manly. I might get type-cast. There's so much to think about. Little did I know.

CLARE. You never stop, do you?

KATE. What for? Nothing's happening. Well, not quite nothing. Can you keep a secret? You and about five other people? Mr. Chenowith gave me his card.

CLARE. What?

KATE. Sure. I'm going to meet him for a drink after my audition ... at the Chanticleer. I thought that would cheer you up.

CLARE. It does.

KATE. See, Edie spilled a drink, I wiped it up and he gave me his card. It was simple as that. Well, we had a sort of quick talk ... I made sure Vicky wasn't around. I had to talk fast ... faster than I usually talk. It was a real treat. I don't know where you were, but I was having a great time.

(The toilet flushes.)

KATE. What's so funny? Will you quit it?

CLARE. Oh, help.

KATE. Is that it? What Vicky was so pissed about just now? Shit. I am so slow.

CLARE. Why me? Oh, God...

KATE. Does she know? Will you quit it?

CLARE. It doesn't make sense. Nothing makes sense.

KATE. Does she know? ... About this?

CLARE. Shhhh ...

KATE. Shh, yourself. Does she?

CLARE. Shhhh, shhhhh ...

KATE. You already said that.

CLARE. Shhh, shhhh ...

KATE. I'm sorry ... I didn't quite get that and neither did the studio audience.

CLARE. Shhhh ...

KATE. Shhhh, shhhh ...

CLARE. Shhhh ... shut ... shhhhhh ...

CLARE. Shuuuu ... shhhut. Keep your mouth shut.

(CLARE and KATE roar with laughter. DANUSHA and EDIE are amused. CHARLENE has mixed feelings in the bathroom.)

CLARE. She was right. Vicky was right. I can't stand it. Maybe I ought to tell her so she knows what it feels like.

KATE. Shhhhh ...

CLARE. *(recovering)* I hope you have the time of your life.

KATE. You know, we were never close, but I always liked you.

CLARE. Shh ... I always liked you, too.

CHARLENE. Don't.

EDIE. I like you, too.

(There is a pause. Then KATE rises.)

KATE. Shit. I have to go. Do you know what time it is? I'll take a taxi. *(She grabs her bag and closes her locker.)* Do you think if I spend the night with him that I'll look any different in the morning?

CLARE. No.

KATE. I'm the only woman I know who can't wait to be over thirty.

CHARLENE. Will you get outa here?

KATE. Isn't anyone going to wish me good luck? *(She exits.)*

EDIE. Good luck.

CLARE. *(to CHARLENE)* You still want to stay for me?

CHARLENE. Yeah.

CLARE. I wouldn't blame you if you changed your mind.

CHARLENE. Forget it. Get some rest. That's all ya need. Things'll be different tomorrow---they always are.

CLARE. Yeah.

CHARLENE. Listen...about Kate...she didn't do nothin'. I talked her into it.

CLARE. It's probably the best thing that's happened to her since she got here. You know, I don't think she's told her parents where she's working. Yesterday she muttered something about what she would do if her father suddenly walked in for lunch. I think they still think she's a guidette at NBC.

CHARLENE. And she says I keep secrets. What a case.

CLARE. Listen...about the Rolls Royce...maybe I could explain things to him...that it was all my fault.

CHARLENE. No, honey...it's too---listen, ya just forget it. It hadda happen sometime. Better now than after a coupla years.

CLARE. Yeah.

CHARLENE. I know ya wouldn't a told Greg about him on purpose. Ya just forget I ever said anythin' about anythin', okay? Ya go ahead and do things the way ya think is best for ya.

CLARE. I don't know what that way is any more.
CHARLENE. You'll find out.
CLARE. Charlene? I'm glad I know you.
CHARLENE. It's mutual, I'm sure. I gotta go ta work.
CLARE. Thanks for taking over.
CHARLENE. I ain't takin' over. Just helpin' out. See ya
Monday.
CLARE. Yeah.

(CHARLENE exits.)

CLARE. *(to DANUSHA)* Are you alright?
DANUSHA. I'm fine.
CLARE. You've had quite a day.
DANUSHA. Yes.
CLARE. *(Looks at EDIE.)* We all have, I guess.
DANUSHA. We are all the same.

(CLARE looks at DANUSHA.)

EDIE. Well, I gotta go.
CLARE. You did really well today.
EDIE. Thanks. I wanta be a good waitress...like you
said. Keep good checks.
CLARE. Keep good checks...yes.
EDIE. Well, have a nice weekend. And thanks for the
underwear.
CLARE. Happy birthday.
EDIE. See ya. *(She exits.)*
CLARE. We are all the same?
DANUSHA. We all went out.

CLARE. I am so confused.

DANUSHA. He who follows life with his mind...Exits through his mouth.
He who follows life with his nose...Exits through his heart.

CLARE. What?

DANUSHA. Yes, I said that right...

CLARE. I don't know.

DANUSHA. But you do. That's just it. You do know. Here. *(She touches her sternum.)*

CLARE. Here?

DANUSHA. Yes. All you'll ever need to know.

CLARE. But that doesn't make any sense.

DANUSHA. I'm having a baby. Does that make sense? There are some things you know you have to do. There are no reasons why. You just know...and you do them.

CLARE. Can I ask you something? Have you ever heard yourself say something and it's like it's not you speaking... but somehow, you know you're there?

DANUSHA. Yes, many times.

CLARE. I put a sign up on the bulletin board so my husband could earn some money coaching the girls who sing ... and I remember, I was pushing in the thumb tack and I heard myself say, "You're not just putting up a sign. You're doing something else." Do you know what I'm talking about?

DANUSHA. Yes.

CLARE. It was like I knew it---way deep down. Something was going to happen if I went through with it. Things were going fall apart...and I couldn't stop myself. And I didn't, did I?

DANUSHA. Yes.

CLARE. I wanted them to, didn't I?

(DANUSHA feels faint and heads for the john.)

CLARE. Are you alright?

DANUSHA. Yes.

(DANUSHA goes into the john.)

CLARE. Are you sure?

DANUSHA. It's nothing...just dizzy.

CLARE. *(Looks at herself in the mirror and takes off her wig.)* Danusha? I never told anybody this before---not even Charlene---but right after Greg and I met...when I didn't go to Europe with Jessy Martin...I was waving 'goodbye' and I knew I should have been on the boat beside her. That nothing was going to turn out the way I wanted it to. For a split second I knew it all. Just like with the bulletin board---only that time I didn't follow through. I was only nineteen. What was I supposed to do...not get married because I'd had a feeling? I thought as I got older things would change...that feeling would go away---and if it didn't...well, I'd find a way to fix it, see?

DANUSHA. Yes, I see.

CLARE. Bury it. Get rid of it...something. I can't, can I?

(RHONDA enters. CLARE is taken by surprise. They stare at each other. CLARE starts to speak...can't quite.)

RHONDA. Somethin' on your mind?

(CLARE turns to her locker and starts getting undressed.
RHONDA waits.)

CLARE. This is ridiculous. This is really ridiculous.

RHONDA. What's that?

CLARE. Oh, nothing. We...uh...we can't go on meeting like this.

RHONDA. Oh yeah?

CLARE. I mean...I know...about you...about you and Greg. That you've been...seeing...each other.

RHONDA. Hey---far out.

CLARE. *(half embarrassed)* Oh...not so far out. You're really only one of many.

RHONDA. Speak for yourself.

CLARE. *(Turns back to her locker, takes out the man's shirt she wore to work.)* Is...it anything...serious?

RHONDA. Well, we're goin' back ta Vegas, if that's what ya mean. Soon as we cut the demo. Don't look so hurt. You can come with us.

CLARE. Oh, no thank you. I don't believe I will. Not this time. *(Hangs her shirt on her locker door.)*

RHONDA. It really wouldn't be a good idea, now... would it?

CLARE. Not really. Not under the circumstances.

RHONDA. Hey, man...ya gotta be kiddin'. What circumstances? I ain't done nothin' wrong. Not like you think. I just got what he needs ta stay high.

CLARE. What?

RHONDA. Grass, man---acid, coke, speed---even smack when he wants it and it looks like that's just a matter of time.

CLARE. What are you talking about?

RHONDA. Right now he's heavy into coke and flirtin' with speedballs.

CLARE. How heavy?

RHONDA. Well, he prefers it ta gettin' laid, now...don't he? That's gotta tell ya somethin'. Ya been gettin' your head all messed up over nothin'. Hey, man...he don't wanta be saved.

CLARE. How would you know?

RHONDA. Cause I know where he's livin'. You only know where he's from.

CLARE. You don't know the first thing about him...or anybody else, for that matter. Look at yourself. You aren't even here. The best thing that ever happened to him was when the group broke up...what do you want to pull them back together for? To watch them fall apart? It isn't fun, Rhonda. I've been through it. They aren't a side show. They're human beings.

RHONDA. Do they get a prize?

CLARE. What?

RHONDA. Does that make em special?

CLARE. Maybe. Maybe we're all something special.

RHONDA. Save your breath.

CLARE. Is it such a terrible thing being decent?

RHONDA. Bein' what? It's his life, ain't it?

CLARE. You didn't have to help him destroy it.

RHONDA. Hey, man - I didn't help him destroy nothin'. You're the one's been payin' for it. Don't talk ta me about bein' decent.

(CLARE watches RHONDA for a long time. RHONDA starts to

back down. CLARE doesn't flinch.)

RHONDA. What ya lookin at?

(CLARE doesn't answer.)

RHONDA. Ya gonna tell your old man ta shape up or you're cuttin off his allowance? Hey, man...he ain't made up his own mind in so long now, it's scary. He don't wanta know from choices. He wants one thing and I got it. What d'ya think he's been tryin' ta tell ya? He don't wanta go back ta no farm. Start a restaurant. Shit...I bet if you play your cards right...he'll let ya have it...sign it over...instead of alimony, dig it? Hey, I mean...ya put your time in ya oughta get what's comin' to ya, right?

CLARE. What's comin' to me? Rhonda, what's coming to me already came.

RHONDA. Yeah?

CLARE. Yeah.

RHONDA. Well, it don't look ta me like it amounted ta much.

CLARE. No, it wouldn't.

RHONDA. What's so funny?

CLARE. You're so young.

RHONDA. I got me a group, don't I?

CLARE. A group of what?

RHONDA. Get off my back. *(Exits, slamming the door.)*

(CLARE puts on her coat. DANUSHA enters from the john.)

DANUSHA. Whew. I think the worst is over. Nothing

more can come up.

CLARE. *(Takes in the locker room and then looks at DANUSHA.)* I may not be here on Monday.

DANUSHA. Thank God.

CLARE. I may not be here on Monday. *(Goes to her locker, puts on her parka and picks up her bag. She looks at DANUSHA.)* Thanks. *(She exits.)*

DANUSHA. *(Gets her coat out of her locker, puts it on and looks at herself in the mirror.)* Ah, such is so.

END OF ACT III

PROPERTIES

ACT I

ONSTAGE PRESET:

1 rug
2 stools
SR bench
    on:
            1 tray w/2 dirty glasses
            1 dirty glass
            Newspaper
SL bench
    on:
            1 plate w/bits of old cheese and bread
            1 full ashtray
            1 dirty glass
    under:2 dirty glasses
    on floor, US end: 1 box glitter
1 heater
1 long extension chord
2 side chairs
1 card table
    on:
            1 lighted make-up mirror (plugged to long
               extension chord)
            1 full ashtray
            2 dirty glasses
            1 glue tube
            Packages of sequins (open)

Tube of glitter
1 bag jelly beans w/6 blanched almonds (open)
1 box kleenex
3 dirty kleenex
1 waste basket
1 sink
1 medicine chest w/mirror
Kleenex in hole in wall
In toilet: 1 glass 'throw up'

LOCKERS:

#1   empty
#2   **CLARE**
       costume
       1 box bobby pins, hairpins, safety pins
       1 can hairspray
       1 small mirror on door
       1 open package Trident Cinnamon gum (1 stick)
       1 matchbox
          in: earrings, necklace, 1 pen
#3   **CHARLENE**
       costume
       2 wooden hangers
       1 box bobby pins, large safety pins
#4   empty *(May be opened, so dress.)*
#5   **KATE**
       costume
       extra red shoes
       hairbrush w/elastic bands, bobby pins
       1 tan box w/bobby pins, hairpins, safety pins

     1 make-up bag w/makeup
     pen
     kleenex (box & loose)
     2 hangers
     bumblebee for stockings

#6   **CHRYSTAL/EDIE**
     costume (shoes too big)
     2 hangers
     1 pr. white foam falsies
     glitter
     magazine cutouts
     empty purse on floor of locker

#7   **VICKY**
     costume
     extra clothes & white shoes
     several TV fan magazines
     2 religious Xmas cards & Pictures of kids

#8   **DANUSHA**
     costume & spikes
     stickers (on already)
     perfume oil & deodrant
     hairspray

#9   Dressing
     1 hairbrush - (VICKY)
     costume

#10 empty

#11 **RHONDA**
     costume
     kleenex
     ponds cold cream

#12 Dressing
     costume & Kate's stockings

OFFSTAGE RIGHT

1 glass ½ full Postum *(CLARE)*
1 cigarette box
    in:
            cartons Trues, Kents, Marlboro, Salem
            1 money box w/money
            1 box w/matches
            1 gun cigarette lighter

PERSONAL PROPS

CLARE: 1 recipe book w/lots of loose recipes
            1 hairbrush
            1 bag w/wig
            1 bag w/'new' makeup
            1 wallet w/dimes (or change purse)
            dressing for purse
            money (tips)
            checks
CHARLENE: 2 bobby pins
            1 rat tail comb
            1 change purse w/dimes
            small package kleenex
            makeup
            dressing for purse
            tips
            1 pen & checks
KATE: 1 copy St. Joan
            dressing
            Mr. Chenowith card
            tips
            1 pen & checks

EDIE: 1 slip paper 'Mr. Minetti'
1 wrist watch
1 pen
1 hairbrush
false fingernails
1 small pack kleenex
1 package sugarless gum
dressing for purse
checks

VICKY: 1 wallet w/10 dollar bill, dimes, pennies
1 change purse
1 piece paper w/doctor's excuse
lots of packs of matches
mess (empty True packs, gum wrappers)
tips
1 pen & checks

DANUSHA: 1 notebook
makeup bag w/ makeup
hairbrush
kleenex
dressing
3 singles
1 pen & checks

RHONDA: 1 makeup bag w/makeup
1 package Trues w/5 joints, nasal douche
cigarette box

HENRI: 1 package Kents, matches
omelet bowl/whisk

JESUS: 1 small white pad w/pencil

CHARLENE: 1 large ring

CHEF: 2 linen towels

ACT II

ONSTAGE PRESET:

Work Table

1 platter w/3 chicken breast (raw)
1 platter w/2 chop steaks (raw)
1 platter w/4 sirloins, 3 filets (raw)
1 bowl w/12 eggs
1 cookie sheet
    on: 4 metal casseroles w/2 quennelles each
1 container quennelle sauce w/ladle
6 beat up aluminum pie plates
1 pr. tongs
wooden cooking utensils & pounder
several large rags

under:
    5 girls purses
    large garbage can (empty)
    dressing

Locker W/Cutting Board Top

1 bowl w/ few almonds
1 plate french bread for soup
1 bowl parsley flakes
in:
    1 metal casserole w/filet of sole
    1 bowl full of almonds
    2 tongs, spatula, long fork

Grille

10 precooked chopped steaks

Stove

under: *(all precooked)*
    1 sirloin (in pie tin)
    1 chicken (in pie tin)
    1 fillet (in pie tin)
    1 fillet sole w/butter (in metal dish)

1 pan for frying liver (spray Pam)
1 small pan for frying almonds
1 omelet pan
1 large container canned potatoes w/ladle & parsley
1 large container canned peas w/ slotted spoon
1 clean towel on C. oven

under: (in warming oven)
    top shelf:
        2 orders beef wellington
        2 orders newburg in pottery casseroles
        5 metal casseroles w/eggs benedict (no sauce)
    bottom shelf:
        1 metal casserole w/2 quennelles (w/sauce)

near:
    small trash can

Bread Warmers

1 bottle 'oil' (in wine bottle w/ spout)
1 container cooking butter w/parsley (soft)
1 butter brush & 1 wooden spoon
cooking utensils
1 bottle cooking sherry (tea? practical), corked
salt, pepper, garlic salt, seasonings
1 bowl for making omelets (peds polito)
1 whisk (peds polito)
dressing?

in: rolls, enough for 8 bread baskets
on second warmer:
    1 container parsley flakes
    1 container grated cheddar cheese
    1 container sliced mushrooms

Carving Block
Stool

Bain Marie

1 container onion soup w/ladle
1 container lobster bisque w/ladle
1 container mushroom soup w/ladle
1 container brown gravy w/ladle
1 container hollandaise w/ladle
20 soup bowls /SL bowl cont. closed
1 cleaver
1 tasting plate
1 small bowl parsley flakes

Counter

1 nail board w/girls names (1dupe on Jeanette's nail)
1 plain pad paper
1 bowl chopped parsley (SL side)
1 bowl lemon wedges (SL side)
1 box for dupes (SR side)
1 dupe holder
55 plate covers
20 small plates (soup liners)
1 glass ice water

under:
    4 stacks dinner plates
    3 breakable plates
    dressing

Rubber Mat

Salad Bar And Condiment Table

1 large container lettuce
1 container cherry tomatoes
2 stacks salad plates
12 containers for mustard (4 are mostly empty)
12 containers mayo, full
12 ketchup bottles
2 rags for wiping bottles
2 containers house dressing w/ladle
1 container blue cheese dressing w/ladle
Worchestershire sauce, tobasco sauce, steak sauce

1 rubber bowl scraper for filling mustard
tongs & knife
under (in locker):
   1 restaurant size mustard (full)
   1 restaurant size mayo

Coffee Bar

coffee machine w/3 pots full coffee, 1 pot w/½ cup
   Postum, 1 pot hot water
Coffee grounds in basket
12 bread baskets (1 is full of rolls, some partly eaten)
stack of napkins
under:
   several creamers and sugars
   bags of coffee for machine
   coffee filters (open)
   coffee baskets
   dressing

2 Runners
Check Rack W/Checks
Rolling Tray-Wagon

1 menu
6 small trays
1 rag
under: 15 big trays
near: trash can, broom, mop & mop bucket

Overhead rack W/Pots And Pans

Sideboard In Front Of Partition

silverware in tray
napkins
tableclothes
waterglasses
coffee cups and saucers
individual water pitchers for tea and sanka
water pitchers
salt and peppers
ice machine

OFFSTAGE RIGHT:

checks for girls (20 per perf)
extra pens (cover)
6 trays dirty dishes (make up on smaller trays)
1 small tray w/2 dirty soups and liners (CHARLENE)
1 small tray w/shot glass w/olive, napkin (CHARLENE)
1 slip white paper w/food order (KATE)
1 small tray w/drinks and napkins (KATE)
1 large empty tray w/napkin (JESUS)
1 empty bread basket (JESUS)
1 small tray cocktails w/napkins (EDIE)
1 small tray (for coffee) (CHARLENE)
1 small tray (wet) w/ napkins (EDIE)

OFFSTAGE LEFT:

1 small tray w/drinks, napkins (VICKY)
5 checks (VICKY)
1 small tray w/1 drink (VICKY)

DOWN RIGHT:

1 container salad greens to refill bowl (JESUS)
1 container chopped meat (CHEF)
1 plate w/2 pieces liver (raw) (CHEF)
1 container ice (JESUS)
7 large trays
1 stack plate covers (DANUSHA)
12 eggs to refill onstage egg bowl (CHEF)
1 full bottle cooking sherry (CHEF)

DOWN LEFT:

1 open carton "Trues"

ACT III

STRIKE: ashtray SL bench (if there)

RESET: all props and costumes as left in Act I
              stool to Act I spikes

SET: DANUSHA'S shoes, pen, some checks on
              floor DS end of SL bench
              Give her her sox and coat.

OFFSTAGE RIGHT:

10 singles (KATE)
1 bowl hot soup on liner w/2 saltines, spoon (KATE)
1 box 'one size fits all' underpants (EDIE)

1 plate w/salad, fork (partly eaten) (EDIE)
money box from cigarette box
package Trues w/joints, inhaler (RHONDA)

PRESETS

Girls' Lockers - costumes unzipped & unhooked.
   Tights right side out.

#1	empty
#2	CLARE
	PPW - dark blue
	body - left hook hung by crotch
	corset - standing up in back on bottom
	shoes - top shelf (nylon peds in one toe, tights folded in other toe)
	earrings & necklace - in match box top shelf pinbox, matchbox
#3	CHARLENE
	SL-purplebody and corset - right hook (corset by loop, body by crotch)
	stockings - left hook
	shoes - bottom
	ribbon & earrings - top shelf (ribbon left, earrings middle)
	2 empty hangers on bar - 1 wire, 1 wooden
	Check that "breakaway" is in unbroken position.
#4	empty

#5   KATE
              LC - gold
              Body - on hanger by crotch
              corset - left hook
              shoes - on bottom
              brush, crown, ribbon (order from bottom
                  to top) center top shelf
              earrings - on plastic box top shelf R.
              Stockings in ±10.
#6   EDIE
              CW - lavender
              body - right hook
              corset - folded on top shelf
              stockings - slung over center of bar
              empty hanger - on left hook
              2 white pads - on bottom
              Locker latch down to close tight.
#7   VICKY
              PS - red
              body - left hook
              corset & stockings - right hook
              shoes - on bottom with other "stuff"
              jewelry - earrings, necklace, haircombs -
                  box on top shelf
#8   DANUSHA
              CA - light blue
              body - left hook
              corset - standing, bottom behind shoes
              shoes - on bottom
              stockings - back hook, right side
              blue neck ribbon - right hook
              headribbon - preset in purse in makeup
                  case

#9	fake costume - bow
#10	fake - bow & Curran tights - rt. hook
#11	RHONDA
	SS - black
	body - top shelf crotch out
	corset - on top of body, bottom out
	stockings - folded on top of corset
	boots - unzipped, cuffed down, in front of locker, leaning to the left
	garter - top shelf, R
	chocker - curled in right front corner

End Of Act One

1.   Strike **EDIE'S** lavender *body* & *purse* to dressing room. Set street clothes (bra, sweater, skirt, slip & stockings [next to pile], chain in bottom) in locker for Act III. Close locker door.

2.   Strike **DANUSHA'S** coat to dressing room.

3.   Strike **VICKY** to dressing room: shoes from floor, bra from bench, dress & stockings in locker

4.   Strike **CHARLENE** to dressing room: in locker - dress, stockings, slip, bra, boots, bangles, earrings. Close locker.

Top Of Act Two

Set purses onstage under wooden table:
1. Charlene   brown w/chain
2. Clare   green canvas
3. Vicky   yellow & brown leather
4. Kate   large wool colored
5. Danusha   wool color w/ string strap

End Of Act Two

Strike purses to dressing room (DANUSHA'S to KATE)

Top Of Act Three

Reset from Act I & set Act III:
1. KATE'S street shoes SR of stool, front of locker 1.
2. DANUSHA'S shoes, downstage end of SL bench & pen w/shoes.

Act III Checklist

1. CLARE & KATE'S coats on hooks.
2. VICKY'S coat on locker.
3. RHONDA'S coat on nail in back.
4. EDIE'S street clothes set in locker.
5. CHARLENE & EDIE street clothes to dressing room.
5. DANUSHA'S coat struck to dressing room.
6. CHARLENE'S fur in locker.

DAILY

CLARE'S wig styled
stockings
underwear
socks
bras & slips

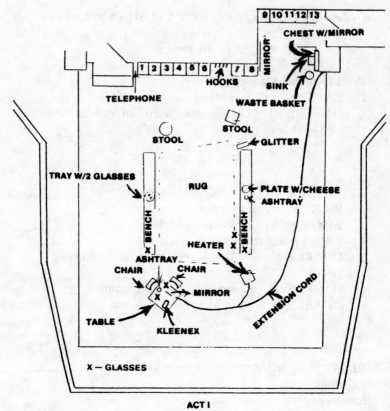

ACT I

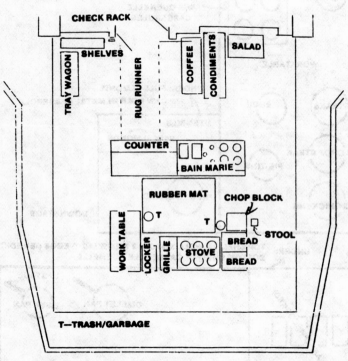

ACT II

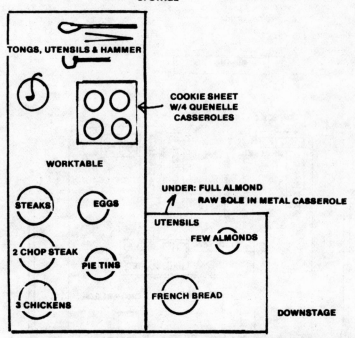

UPSTAGE

TONGS, UTENSILS & HAMMER

COOKIE SHEET
W/4 QUENELLE
CASSEROLES

WORKTABLE

UNDER: FULL ALMOND
RAW SOLE IN METAL CASSEROLE

STEAKS

EGGS

UTENSILS
FEW ALMONDS

2 CHOP STEAK

PIE TINS

3 CHICKENS

FRENCH BREAD

DOWNSTAGE

UNDER: TOP SHELF: 2 WELLINGTON, 2 NEWBURG 5 EGGS BENEDICT
BOTTOM SHELF: 1 CASSEROLE QUENELLE

UPSTAGE

OMELET PAN

LIVER PAN

CHOP STEAKS (PRECOOKED)

PEAS W/SLOTTED
SPOON

POTATOES W/LADLE
OR SPOON

ALMOND PAN

GRILLE

STOVE

ACT II

DOWNSTAGE

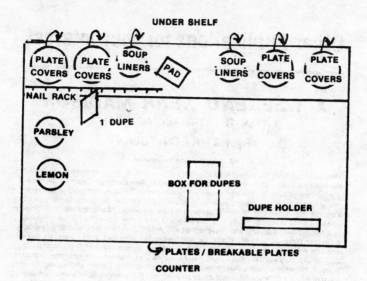

UNDER SHELF

PLATE COVERS · PLATE COVERS · SOUP LINERS · PAD · SOUP LINERS · PLATE COVERS · PLATE COVERS

NAIL RACK

1 DUPE

PARSLEY

LEMON

BOX FOR DUPES

DUPE HOLDER

PLATES / BREAKABLE PLATES

COUNTER

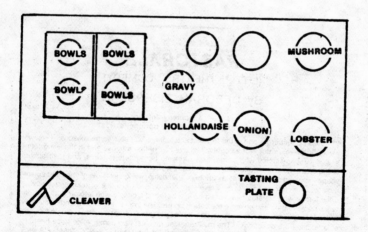

BOWLS · BOWLS

BOWLS · BOWLS

GRAVY

MUSHROOM

HOLLANDAISE · ONION · LOBSTER

CLEAVER

TASTING PLATE

BAIN MARIE

ACT II

Other Publications for Your Interest

A WEEKEND NEAR MADISON
(LITTLE THEATRE—COMIC DRAMA)
By KATHLEEN TOLAN

2 men, 3 women—Interior

This recent hit from the famed Actors Theatre of Louisville, a terrific ensemble play about male-female relationships in the 80's, was praised by *Newsweek* as "warm, vital, glowing . . . full of wise ironies and unsentimental hopes". The story concerns a weekend reunion of old college friends now in their early thirties. The occasion is the visit of Vanessa, the queen bee of the group, who is now the leader of a lesbian/feminist rock band. Vanessa arrives at the home of an old friend who is now a psychiatrist hand in hand with her naif-like lover, who also plays in the band. Also on hand are the psychiatrist's wife, a novelist suffering from writer's block; and his brother, who was once Vanessa's lover and who still loves her. In the course of the weekend, Vanessa reveals that she and her lover desperately want to have a child—and she tries to persuade her former male lover to father it, not understanding that he might have some feelings about the whole thing. *Time Magazine* heard "the unmistakable cry of an infant hit . . . Playwright Tolan's work radiates promise and achievement."   (#25051)

(Royalty, $60–$40.)

PASTORALE
(LITTLE THEATRE—COMEDY)
By DEBORAH EISENBERG

3 men, 4 women—Interior
(plus 1 or 2 bit parts and 3 optional extras)

"Deborah Eisenberg is one of the freshest and funniest voices in some seasons."—Newsweek. Somewhere out in the country Melanie has rented a house and in the living room she, her friend Rachel who came for a weekend but forgets to leave, and their school friend Steve (all in their mid-20s) spend nearly a year meandering through a mental landscape including such concerns as phobias, friendship, work, sex, slovenliness and epistemology. Other people happen by: Steve's young girlfriend Celia, the virtuous and annoying Edie, a man who Melanie has picked up in a bar, and a couple who appear during an intense conversation and observe the sofa is on fire. The lives of the three friends inevitably proceed and eventually draw them, the better prepared perhaps by their months on the sofa, in separate directions. "The most original, funniest new comic voice to be heard in New York theater since Beth Henley's 'Crimes of the Heart.'"—N.Y. Times. "A very funny, stylish comedy."—The New Yorker. "Wacky charm and wayward wit."—New York Magazine. "Delightful."—N.Y. Post. "Uproarious . . . the play is a world unto itself, and it spins."—N.Y. Sunday Times.   (#18016)

(Royalty, $50–$35.)

Other Publications for Your Interest

TALKING WITH . . .
(LITTLE THEATRE)
By JANE MARTIN

11 women—Bare stage

Here, at last, is the collection of eleven extraordinary monologues for eleven actresses which had them on their feet cheering at the famed Actors Theatre of Louisville—audiences, critics and, yes, even jaded theatre professionals. The mysteriously pseudonymous Jane Martin is truly a "find", a new writer with a wonderfully idiosyncratic style, whose characters alternately amuse, move and frighten us always, however, speaking to use from the depths of their souls. The characters include a baton twirler who has found God through twirling; a fundamentalist snake handler, an ex-rodeo rider crowded out of the life she has cherished by men in 3-piece suits who want her to dress up "like Minnie damn Mouse in a tutu"; an actress willing to go to any length to get a job; and an old woman who claims she once saw a man with "cerebral walrus" walk into a McDonald's and be healed by a Big Mac. "Eleven female monologues, of which half a dozen verge on brilliance."—London Guardian. "Whoever (Jane Martin) is, she's a writer with an original imagination."—Village Voice. "With Jane Martin, the monologue has taken on a new poetic form, intensive in its method and revelatory in its impact."—Philadelphia Inquirer. "A dramatist with an original voice . . . (these are) tales about enthusiasms that become obsessions, eccentric confessionals that levitate with religious symbolism and gladsome humor."—N.Y. Times. *Talking With . . .* is the 1982 winner of the American Theatre Critics Association Award for Best Regional Play.   (#22009)

(Royalty, $60-$40.
If individual monologues are done separately: Royalty, $15-$10.)

HAROLD AND MAUDE
(ADVANCED GROUPS—COMEDY)
By COLIN HIGGINS

9 men, 8 women—Various settings

Yes: *the Harold and Maude!* This is a stage adaptation of the wonderful movie about the suicidal 19 year-old boy who finally learns how to truly *live* when he meets up with that delightfully whacky octogenarian, Maude. Harold is the proverbial Poor Little Rich Kid. His alienation has caused him to attempt suicide several times, though these attempts are more cries for attention than actual attempts. His peculiar attachment to Maude, whom he meets at a funeral (a mutual passion), is what saves him—and what captivates us. This new stage version, a hit in France directed by the internationally-renowned Jean-Louis Barrault, will certainly delight both afficionados of the film and new-comers to the story. "Offbeat upbeat comedy."—Christian Science Monitor.   (#10032)

(Royalty, $60-$40.)

14156

THE LUNCH GIRLS

by
Leigh Curran

Samuel French, Inc.

About the Author...

LEIGH CURRAN...

...began her career as an actress, appearing on Broadway in HOW NOW, DOW JONES, as well as Off Off Broadway, in regional theatre and on television, in specials, series, and commercials. She can be seen in the films: REDS, A LITTLE SEX, and I NEVER PROMISED YOU A ROSE GARDEN. THE LUNCH GIRLS is her first play. Her second is ALTERATIONS.